Legacy of a Frozen Scream

Glad you enjoyed my book, Izzy!
God bless and keep you.

Daniel D Doty

Excerpts From Reader Reviews

Legacy of a Frozen Scream had my attention from the first page. I enjoyed the author's writing style, the fact I didn't need a spreadsheet to keep track of multiple layers of characters, and the believability of the story. The mystery aspect held my attention to the very end, as I could easily see the story going in several different directions. I hope this is the beginning of a series as I think "Pastor Dave" could have quite a following.

Ann Reeves, Library Director

A page-turner from start to finish, Daniel Doty creates an unexpected mystery through the eyes of flawed, but loveable Pastor David Lee Brady. Alongside the mystery of Sonny's death, Doty explores the complicated roles a modern-day pastor must navigate. Terrific read with a surprise ending.

Erika Collins, Teacher

If there is such a thing as a charming mystery novel, *Legacy of a Frozen Scream*, is certainly one! I was captivated from the first chapter. This novel written about a pastor by a pastor had a lot of great meaningful moments that were touching. The author's detail brought the book to life, kept me turning the pages to solve the mystery to the very end...

Karen Waldrop, fiction connoisseur

Legacy of a Frozen Scream is an exceptional book. Author Daniel D. Doty is a gifted creative writer, and his detailed and descriptive writing style whisks you away into the middle of every scene. The mystery of Sonny's death is one that kept me on my toes through the entire book. Every twist and turn is one that I didn't see coming. As this mystery unravels, you get a peek into the life and mind of a rural Midwest pastor. If you like mystery novels or are interested in getting into the life and mind of a pastor, this is the book for you.

Rev. Megan Hoenig

Legacy of a Frozen Scream

Daniel D. Doty

Text and artwork copyright © 2021 by Daniel D. Doty

All rights reserved.

No portion of this book may be reproduced, stored in a retrieval system, or transmitted in any form or by any means—electronic, mechanical, photocopying, recording, scanning, or other—except for brief quotations in critical reviews or articles without the prior written permission of the author.

Author's note: This novel is a work of fiction. Names characters, places, and incidents are either products of the author's imagination or used fictitiously. All characters are fictional, and any similarity to people living or dead is purely coincidental.

Library of Congress number applied for.

ISBN 979-8-9852019-0-1

Dedication

A third-grade teacher in the Clarion Public School system in Clarion, Iowa, offered a deeply troubled student encouragement for writing what is now a long forgotten short story. Those encouraging words, quietly nurtured throughout my life was the incentive that inspired *Legacy of a Frozen Scream*. (See Postscript.)

I dedicate this book to that teacher.

Acknowledgments

Thank you to the following people who contributed in important ways to this book:

Catherine Argo, Mark Barra, Jennie Brown, Hannah Chapman, Paul Clark, Julie Clemens, Jim Coffman, Darren Evans, Beverly Doty, Jon Doty, Jamie Jones, Mike Jones, Fred Larsen, Norlyn McCormick, Jerry McDowell, Robert E. Naugle, Chris Nichols, Julie Nichols, Kelly Nichols, Pam Plumer, Dramane Taylor, Lin Walkington and Cindy Wondercheck.

Thank you also to several police officers who contributed but wished to remain anonymous.

Legacy of a Frozen Scream

by Daniel D. Doty

Chapter 1

Pastor David Lee Brady would have a difficult time getting others to accept his notion of what made up a great morning walk. The ingredients for today were cold air, falling snow, and darkness except for the streetlights. The late October snow provided a nature lover like himself with a perfect start to a new day.

Dave, a spry sixty-two-year-old man, moved rapidly through a circle of light provided by a streetlamp. The sight of the beautiful white flakes swept him back in time. As a boy, his grandfather would take him for walks in the woods during a snowfall. Deep in the trees, Gramps would stop, put an index finger to his lips, and cup his other hand behind an ear. In the silence, young Dave became conscious of the quiet but distinct whisper of snowflakes as they showered the surrounding winter wonderland.

Now, as the cold air bit at his cheeks, Dave shoved his hands into the pockets of his jacket and continued down the quiet street. On one side of the road, there was a cornfield ready for the harvest, and on the other side of the road was a row of smaller, older homes. As a tribute to his grandfather, he breathed in the cold, crisp air while his ears enjoyed a unique musical piece. The faint patter of tiny ice crystals alighting upon the trees and shrubs were musical notes that together performed a divine adagio. He enjoyed thinking of himself as a musician within this orchestra, the crunching and squeaking of each footfall the percussion for the symphony.

Dave would soon enter his favorite section of his morning walk. There were fewer houses, no streetlights, and trees lined both sides of the roadway. In the warmer months, wildflowers splattered the shallow ditches with color. As the beauty of the snow swirled all around, his mind was preoccupied with other things. A week and a half ago, his congregation had completed the construction of a ground-level fellowship hall. The building—fully paid for—was put to use for the first-time last Sunday. The new facility would be used by both the congregation and the Baunsee community for decades to come, a matter of legitimate pride for church members and a feather in his own hat.

But despite the accomplishment, and the new community program already in play, destructive self-doubts—an aftermath of a troubled childhood—bubbled below the surface. Even after all these years, guilt weighed on him for repeated failures to protect his mother from the repeated assaults of his drunken father. After more than a decade of good counseling, Dave realized the brutal experiences when he was a child that convinced him he was a worthless piece of garbage, were no longer his truth. The words persisted, still whispered in his ear, but had lost their ability to govern his behavior.

The barking of a nearby dog lifted Dave above thoughts of his troubled childhood and brought a smile to his face. His wife, Barb, who only accompanied him on his walks in the summer months, once told him she could monitor the progress of his walk around the village by listening to the dogs sound out their respective alarms.

Dave slowed his pace as he passed the emu enclosure, an unusual attraction for the tiny town. The fencing and shed were silhouettes, black shapes against a narrow streak of yellow along the eastern horizon. He enjoyed seeing the birds, now invisible within their darkened surroundings. Off in the distance another dog barked. The snowflakes were smaller now, less fluffy, and intermittent gusts of light wind were altering the earthward course of the miniature ice crystals.

Then a scream pierced the air. A long, unearthly scream.

A shiver crawled down his spine. Dave stopped dead in his tracks. Motionless, he listened, but heard nothing, saw nothing. All around was blackness, falling snow, and the accustomed sounds of pre-dawn in a small Illinois community.

4

From another direction, a car door slammed, interrupting the silence. An engine started. But Dave's ears were attuned to what had made that blood-curdling cry. A coyote? Local coyotes made a variety of sounds, some of them human-like, but he had never heard the animals utter such a chilling shriek.

Less than a hundred feet away, a car made its way toward Dave, the headlights blinding him. The red SUV crept closer and stopped. The streetlight revealed an attractive middle-aged woman with blonde hair. Dave smiled. On most mornings, Micky acknowledged his presence with a quick smile and a wave.

"Love your hat, Pastor," she teased in sweet feminine tones. "That oughta keep your head warm and dry!"

The thin, white cotton Gilligan-style hat covered Dave's receding hairline. It was almost soaked through. Other than that, he wore seasonable outer clothing—a dark green wind breaker bulked out by the sweatshirt beneath, black sweatpants with two narrow white stripes down the outside of each leg, and white tennis shoes, their soil stains offering evidence of his summer work in the garden.

"Isn't this somethin'?" Micky continued. "It's not even November."

Dave nodded, distracted. "Did you hear that horrible scream?" His tension-laced voice communicated his deep concern.

"It's just a coyote," Micky said.

He peered into her eyes. "Are you sure?"

Yes. "We hear them all the time out here on the edge of town. They can make the most god-awful sounds."

Unconvinced, Dave peered off into the surrounding darkness, then he turned back to Micky. He didn't want to call his friend's judgment into question again for fear of offending her, so he changed the subject. "What've you heard from the kids?"

Though not members of Dave's church, the previous year he had conducted the wedding ceremony for Micky's daughter, her only child, and her fiancé, at Micky's home. Both the daughter and her husband were making a career of the military.

"My son-in-law is still at Great Lakes, and my daughter has been moved on assignment to Hawaii," she replied.

But Dave wasn't listening. He just couldn't get the horrible outcry from his mind.

"Don't look so concerned," Micky continued. "It's a temporary assignment. They're used to being apart—it goes with their jobs. They'll be okay."

Dave forced himself back into the moment, trying to sound enthusiastic. "If I were you, I'd jump on the Hawaii thing."

"I'm already on it." A bright smile accompanied Micky's reply. For the next two or three minutes she described her computer search for airline tickets. "There are good deals out there," she concluded, "but ya gotta look for 'em. Well, it's been nice talkin' to you, Pastor Dave, but I better go or I'll be late."

Dave offered an anxious half-smile and stepped back. "Hope you have a good one."

Micky reached out the window and gently grasped his forearm. "It's just a coyote, Pastor Dave, just the crazy cry of a coyote. No reason for alarm."

"Okay, okay! I'll try to shut it off." He smiled.

Micky said her goodbyes and drove away.

She's probably right, Dave thought, and relaxed in anticipation of the snow-covered trees along the next section of his hike. The pause to talk to his friend had intensified the chill, and he increased his speed to warm himself up.

Within seconds another pitiful shriek stopped him cold. His eyes searched the landscape. Barely a hundred feet to his right was an old one-story brick home. He thought the cry came from that direction, but he could see nothing in the darkness, heard only the hushed sounds of earth receiving a premature winter coat.

Alarm bells in his head compelled him to leave the road and step into the yard, which slanted downward away from the blacktop, and behind the house fell more precipitously into a tree-filled ravine. Ahead, close to the house, Dave spied a snow-covered mound. *It moved*, he thought. He rushed forward and kneeled beside it. He brushed the snow aside and found an arm covered in the sleeve of a light jacket. Moving fast, he brushed the snow from around a young man's head. Even in the darkness, he recognized the face.

"Sonny! Sonny!" he shouted. "What happened?"

Chest flat against the ground, the twenty-year-old's head moved and from his mouth came another scream, different from the previous shrieks Dave had heard.

"Aaaaddrrrrrrrrr—!"

Dave moved quickly, brushing more of the snow away from Sonny's head and upper body. Removing his windbreaker, he threw it over the motionless form, shouting for Tina, the young man's mother.

"Shit! Shit! Shit!" The expletives burst from Dave's mouth as he jumped to his feet, but then his foot caught on something solid beneath the snow and he fell hard on one knee. Recovering his footing, Dave scrambled up and ran to the front door of the home. Tina's car wasn't in the driveway. He beat on the door with one fist while turning the knob with his other hand. The lights were on. Pushing the door open, he shouted for a response but was met with silence.

Unchallenged, he stepped inside. A faint but distinct odor of marijuana greeted his nostrils. The place had been trashed. Chairs were knocked over, an upended coffee table had two broken legs, a couch had been pushed askew, and trash covered the floor. Ignoring the mess, Dave stuck to the need of the moment, found a phone, and pecked out 9-1-1 with fumbling fingers. "Need an ambulance . . . someone's hurt bad . . . found him outside in the snow! Hurry!"

Despite Dave's garbled attempts to communicate, the 911 operator made a simultaneous radio call, then asked for more information.

Dave supplied the necessary information, refused to stay on the phone as he was asked, and went back outside. He knelt beside the helpless young man and brushed the snow away from his head and face again. Then he leaned close to his ear and told him to hang on, an ambulance was on the way. He sat upright and breathed a prayer.

What should I do, he thought? Mind in a muddle, he couldn't think straight. Dave had not taken a first-aid class in years. Should he use his body to warm the kid?

"Blankets!" he shouted. How stupid of him not to think of that while he was in the house. He hurried back inside, pulled the covers off the first bed he found, and ran back to Sonny. He threw the blankets over the boy as he knelt to his side.

"Hang on, Sonny," he said. "Help is on the way!"

9

In the light of the breaking dawn, he searched Sonny's face for any sign of movement. He saw none but noticed three deep gashes on Sonny's cheek.

Until he heard a siren approach, Dave offered Sonny encouraging words, praying for the boy, for the boy's mother, for help to come. The brighter light allowed Dave to see more. He took a closer look at the gashes on Sonny's face, but also saw blood matting the back of the boy's head. He froze, then looked at his hands. His fingers were stained with blood. Shuddering, he scooped up snow to wash it off and then wiped his hands on his gray sweatshirt.

The scream of the siren could be heard in the distance, and it intensified with every passing second. A few moments later, the ambulance crew pulled up and emerged from their vehicle.

"Is he breathing?" Jim Sandmeyer called out. As he waddled through the snow toward them.

"Yes. That's how I found him." Dave stood, backed away. There's blood on the back of his head," he exclaimed. "I think he's hurt bad."

Jim's balding head was hidden under a Chicago Cubs baseball hat. He had been a well-respected community leader for decades, smoked a pipe, and fought bad knees. With effort, he kneeled beside the body, assessed the situation, and, failing to see Sonny's chest move, barked out an order.

A younger EMT retrieved equipment from the ambulance, while Jim tended to Sonny.

"Dave!" a familiar voice shouted, and Dave turned to see his wife's car come to a stop on the edge of the lawn.

He hurried over. *Just what I need right now,* he thought, *another lecture about bringing my cell phone when I go for walks.*

What's goin' on?" Barb exclaimed. "I heard the ambulance and it scared me to death! Are you all right?"

"I'm fine," he said, "but somethin's happened to Sonny."

"Sonny Wigg? Will he be all right? Where's his mom?"

He shrugged. "Sonny's hurt and Tina's not here."

"Can you come home?"

"Can't right now," he replied. "They'll wanna ask me questions. I'll come home when I can."

"Why don't you just give them your name and our address and let me take you home?"

He scowled, peeved by the interference. Shock and guilt were not the only things doing a number on Dave. Barb's questioning, on top of the pervasive effects of the biting, wet cold, self-reproach, and the shocking situation, pushed him over the edge. Without a word, he turned away from the car and retreated back into the yard. Barb drove off.

Three neighbors were standing on the edge of the lawn. A sheriff's deputy, Chris, had also arrived. Dave knew the deputy's mom from church. He had joined the sheriff's office soon after arriving back in the States following a tour in Afghanistan. The young man had been with the department less than six months.

In a few short minutes, the EMTs had put a neck brace on Sonny, bandaged his head, strapped him to a backboard, started an IV, and administered CPR. Earlier Dave had heard them say Sonny had a pulse. He was relieved about that but concerned because they were in such a hurry to get him into the ambulance. Dave stepped forward to help.

Jim turned to Dave and said, "Did he say anything?"

"Nothing intelligible. He just cried out, real loud, two or three times."

As they approached the ambulance, the deputy joined in to help the crew. They fastened the Gurney to the floor of the ambulance and closed the doors.

Deputy Chris looked at Jim and demanded, "Where's Greg? He shoulda got here before I did." Greg Anderson was the village part time policeman.

Jim shrugged and motioned for Chris to follow him. They stepped aside, away from Dave, and had a hurried consultation. The ambulance sped away, lights flashing and sirens blaring. Dave alternately flexed his leg muscles and walked in place in an attempt to warm his feet.

Deputy Chris made his way over. "Did you find him, Pastor?" he asked.

Dave was taken aback. The deputy had never used this formal tone with him. A blank look accompanied his nod.

"Stay right here!" The deputy's firm order left room for no deviation or negotiation. Dave had known Chris since high school, and this last exchange hurt his feelings. But he couldn't dwell on it. Chris was just doing his job.

Deputy Chris turned to the three people who were standing off to the side. "Did any of you see or hear anything?"

They all shook their heads, then one of them said, "I just heard the coyotes."

The deputy ordered them to stay off the lawn but not to go anywhere until he took their names and addresses. The snow, now about four inches, let up a bit.

Deputy Chris opened the driver's side door of the squad car, sat on the seat with one leg extended outside, and talked into his mic. Dave picked up two key words: "crime scene" and "investigator." The deputy finished his call, then grabbed a roll of bright yellow plastic tape from the trunk of his car. As the sound of the siren became lost in the distance, the deputy went to work staking out the perimeter of the crime scene.

Dave heard Barb's voice again and he turned around to see his wife's car pull up. His frozen feet stepped toward her as she held her arm out the passenger window holding his winter coat.

"Thanks," he said sheepishly. He quickly put on the coat and zipped it all the way up. Tucking his hands into the warm side pockets, he found his cell phone. Grateful for the warmth, Dave forced his frozen facial muscles into a stiff smile. "Thanks. Thanks." Then the muscles in his chin quivered, not just from the cold. Dave had an emotional nature and cried easily. He hated this about himself.

"You're welcome," she said. Then she drove off without attempting further conversation.

As he stood alone in the yard, the impact of the morning's events hit him full force. His body shook, afflicted by both emotion and cold. Also, he became conscious of a sharp pain in his right knee. Limping a bit, he turned to the side so no one would see how emotional he had become.

What happened to Sonny? Where was Tina? he thought. If Sonny were to die, it would be so hard on his mother. Not too long ago, Tina's father had told Dave that she had just celebrated three years of being clean and sober.

Sonny's mother had a troubled past, doing drugs and dealing drugs . . . at least that was the village talk. Whatever the facts, Dave recognized the deep scars of a woman with a troubled history. Six years ago, Tina's oldest daughter had lost her life in a car accident. Dave, new in town at the time, had done the funeral service and tried to work with her. She did not open herself up to him. Sonny hadn't finished high school, never held down a steady job, and had been in several minor scrapes with the law, but he was all Tina had left.

Two squad cars—sirens silent but lights flashing—arrived at the scene. The first was an unmarked sheriff SUV with a removable flashing glass bulb on top. Two officers got out. The second car was a Highway Patrol vehicle. After exiting his car, the tall broad-shouldered male officer slipped on an official brown jacket matching his tan uniform and donned a traditional wide-brimmed Highway Patrol hat.

Deputy Chris and the three officers converged on the snow-covered lawn. They did not summon Dave, and he couldn't hear their conversation, but he didn't feel comfortable moving closer. A detective with a graying flattop, wearing a suit and tie, took charge and asked Deputy Chris question after question. The shorter, stockier uniformed officer had coal-black hair and a black toothbrush moustache.

Pastor Dave walked in place to warm his wet feet as he listened to the sound of an eighteen-wheeler grinding its way through town. He listened as it made its way northbound along Highway 99. Before the sound of the engine disappeared, he heard the rig rattle, and then it made a couple of loud bangs as it passed over the rough railroad crossing a short distance north of the village.

Dave looked over at the ramshackle brick house. He breathed a prayer for Tina and Sonny. Concern for the boy and his mom brought a lump to his throat. His knee throbbed with pain. His body, despite the warmth of his jacket, remained frigid.

Finally, the officers motioned for Dave to join them. As Dave approached, Deputy Chris asked, "You okay, Pastor?" His voice was compassionate, no longer the voice of authority.

A shiver accompanied Dave's reply, "Now that you've asked . . . I got chilled to the bone before my wife brought my coat. I'm still cold, and I have to use the bathroom really bad."

The officers chuckled at his frankness and assured him they wouldn't keep him long. A neighbor who had remained to watch what went on stood on the other side of the yellow police tape and offered her bathroom.

On his way to use the neighbor's facilities, Dave noticed the snow had stopped. It began again as he rejoined the officers, but five minutes later it stopped for good.

The investigators were polite and respectful of Dave, yet thorough. The questioning began on the lawn, where they could get a full view of the scene, then, mercifully, in the warmth of the SUV.

16

Once in the vehicle, the deputy with a crewcut placed a small tape recorder between himself and Dave. He recorded the date, October 25, 2005, and stated the three names, and secured Dave's consent to record.

Then came the questions: "What did you see? What did you hear? What time did this happen? How do you know the victim? Who else lives in the house? Do you know where his mother is? Do you know how we can get ahold of her? Did Sonny have enemies?"

When the senior officer found out Dave had been in the house, there were more questions. They were interested in which rooms he had entered, why, and what he touched. When the questioning ended, Dave felt weary. The whole experience had sucked him dry.

At some point, Officer Greg arrived. He showed up in his old, beat-up maroon pickup truck wearing civilian clothes. When the interview concluded, he gave Dave a ride home. Greg had been the town policeman forever. Baunsee's single law enforcement officer snorted when he laughed, lived with his girlfriend, and knew a lot about complex cameras, both mechanical and digital.

Some in town criticized Greg for being a hick, referring to him as Barney Fife, but not to his face of course. While noting Greg's irritating little habits and eccentric nature, Dave regarded him as intelligent and a compassionate public servant, especially when it involved the elderly.

Officer Greg was not disposed to give the unemployed single young adult males of the village a pass on anything.

As Greg pulled onto the highway, a white Class II truck turned onto the street and passed them. "State Crime Lab," Greg said. Gold lettering on the side of the truck confirmed the observation.

Good Lord, Dave thought, *what in the name of God just happened?* He recalled Sonny's face—pale as a sheet of paper—as they'd loaded the gurney into the ambulance. In the first light of morning, he had seen blood—Sonny's blood—streaked across the palm of his hand. The agony of this twice-devastated family, people he knew, cut straight to his soft heart.

Dave spoke in an effort to swallow his emotions. "Know what I felt like while all this was goin' on? I felt like a fish flopping around on a beach somewhere tryin' to get back in the blasted lake! Didn't know what I was doin', what I was supposed to do, how to do it!"

Greg laughed, with a couple of snorts for emphasis. "I'm sure you did just fine." He shrugged his shoulders. "I was in Springfield visiting my mom. I got the call on the way home."

Dave rubbed his sore, stiff knee as he began to tell Greg what had happened. The officer listened carefully and didn't ask any questions. Greg pulled into Dave's driveway and shut off the engine.

Dave, brain-fried, leaned his head against the side window and closed his eyes. "I must've looked like a crazy fool." He sighed.

"Doubt it," Greg replied.

"I felt like a fool," Dave corrected.

"Understood. I don't know anyone who'd feel comfortable in a situation like that."

On any other occasion, Dave and Greg would have talked, but now the air felt heavy.

Dave broke the silence by pressing down on the passenger door handle. Click. He shoved the door open. "Thanks, Greg—for the ride."

"No problem. You did just fine, Pastor." Greg turned the key, and the engine came to life just as Dave pushed the rusted pickup door closed behind him.

Despite the clouds blocking the village from direct sunlight, it generated sufficient warmth to elevate the Midwest to seasonal temperatures. By the time Dave learned that Sonny had died, the snow, all but remnants in shady areas, had disappeared.

Chapter 2

The corridors of Wabaunsee Valley School had a peculiar fragrance of marking pens, ink, glue, paint, paper, books, sweat, and perfume, all mingled with the much stronger odors of cleaning and sanitizing fluids. The students associated the smell with a home away from home, a refuge from parents, stolen kisses in the locker room, failure, bullying, forced labor, or insurmountable challenges.

The junior high section of the building was pregnant with the anticipation of students confined in classrooms under the supervision of their teachers, as both instructors and pupils sensed the eminent sound of the final bell.

Outside of the classrooms, jet-black construction paper cutouts of black cats, bats, jack-o-lanterns, witches, silhouettes of darkened haunted houses, and the like hung on the institutional-gray walls and bulletin boards. Friday was in three days, and the elementary children would wear their Halloween costumes to school, bring treats, and party with their classmates.

The bell shattered the silence, and the relative quiet within each classroom evaporated as the students gathered their things and spilled out of their respective doorways. The halls were flooded with eighty-three boisterous junior high students, some flowing along the corridors one way, while others moved in the opposite direction. Lockers opened and were slammed shut. Students vied for one another's attention:

"Jeremy, wait up!"

"Catherine, come here and look at this!"

"Andy, slow down, dude!"

"Bro, save me a place on the bus!"

The twenty-four-year-old consolidated school building, with separate sections for grade school, junior high, and high school, stood in the middle of nowhere. Surrounded by corn and bean fields, the structure served children and youth from small towns in every direction. The entire student body needed to be bussed or get rides to and from school.

As the hallways emptied, the noise level decreased. Some hurried outside to catch their buses. Others left to meet parents along the drive-through on the side of the school building. Older students went to their cars in the parking lot.

With the exception of teachers finishing up the day's work, or students who were staying for sports or after-school activities or meetings, the student body exited into the welcoming—and sometimes not so welcoming—outside world. Remaining inside were three junior high girls waiting to ambush an enemy. All three wore jeans and sneakers, and had their jackets zipped up, ready for an attack and then flight.

The only sounds in the empty hallway were coming from the other end of the building.

Misty Wendell stood at the sink in the salmon-colored bathroom, the tiled floor stained and wet. The mirror was foggy, and the glass was cracked in one corner. The somewhat-overweight second-year eighth grader wore a tight second-hand rust-colored knit dress just long enough to meet the school dress code. She had put her white windbreaker on over the sweater that she wore to cover the plunging neckline of her dress. The angry fourteen-year-old, incensed over a lifetime of abuse, took delight in dressing as provocatively as school rules would allow. She was running late and would miss her bus if she didn't hurry.

As she scurried out of the restroom, Misty clutched her books and purse tightly. Her wedge platform shoes made a clop-clop sound on the tile floor. But she only made it five steps outside the bathroom door.

Slam!

At a full run, someone had slammed their shoulder into the middle of Misty's back and screamed, "Bitch! You stole my homework."

Misty cried out in pain and bewilderment as her books and purse flew in different directions. She crashed face-first to the hard floor. Shaking, Misty gritted her teeth in anger. There was only one person who would dare such a thing: Kiara.

From day one, Kiara—an equally troubled transfer student from Gillespie—and Misty had clashed. Misty, a loner, had been the undisputed queen of the junior high "bad girls" and saw Kiara as a threat to the control over her domain. The first time the two were without supervision, Misty had attempted to give the new girl a lesson in proper respect. Kiara didn't learn. Misty's relationship with Kiara quickly escalated from epithets, insults, and shunning to dirty tricks. And now to this.

Back on her feet in an instant, Misty turned and saw Kiara's triumphant smile. Fists clenched, she charged at Kiara. She grabbed a lock of Kiara's blonde hair, screamed insults, pushed, shoved, and swatted while her opponent returned the same. The two collided with the lockers. Misty still clung tightly to Kiara's hair and heaved her body weight forward, slamming them both to the floor where they rolled around in a tangle of arms and hair pulls and slaps.

They stood up, heaving and panting, then Kiara lunged at Misty and grabbed her shoulder to hold her steady. Simultaneously she doubled the other hand into a fist and landed a hard blow on Misty's left ear. Misty screamed out in pain. The ringing in her ear was piercing.

"Stop it! Stop it right now!" Mr. Kelly, the speech teacher, yelled as he rushed over and attempted to push the entangled girls apart.

Kiara, who had now gotten in two good licks over her opponent, happily complied and backed off. Mr. Kelly, who was short, slender, and weighed much less than Misty, tried to constrain Misty. Blind with anger, Misty would have run him over had it not been for the intervention of the football coach, Mr. Berry.

In the presence of the powerful, muscular, no-nonsense coach, hostilities between the girls immediately ceased. As everyone took a breath, Kiara flashed Misty an exultant grin. Misty's left ear throbbed.

One of Kiara's two accomplices had vanished; the other, there only for the moral support, stood off to the side, acting like an innocent bystander. The other three witnesses were seventh-grade boys, their eyes wide as they gaped at Misty's tight dress that had worked itself almost up to her waist during the fight. She immediately jerked her elbow from the coach's grasp so she could put herself back together.

Mr. Kelly, Mr. Berry, and Ms. Speas, a new music teacher, instructed the bystanders to get back about their business. Misty and Kiara were immediately marched to the principal's office.

The school secretary stood when they entered. "Sounded like quite a ruckus out there!" she said.

Mr. Kelly answered, "These two girls were at it big time."

The secretary's eyes widened. "Mr. Christianson has left the building for a meeting. I can reach Vice Principal Francis."

While the secretary got on the phone, Mr. Kelly told the girls to sit. Misty and Kiara sat in chairs opposite each other. Kiara was glaring at Misty who was looked down at her hands. She saw scratches, a broken fingernail, and thought of revenge.

A few moments later, Mrs. Francis stormed into the outer office. Her cheeks were flushed, and her curly hair looked unkempt. "What's all this!" she demanded.

"Fighting in the hall," Mr. Kelly answered. "An all-out brawl . . . hitting, hair pulling, and screaming." The other teachers nodded in agreement.

"Were both girls doing the hitting?"

"Yes."

Mrs. Francis turned to the girls and snarled, "In my office!" The girls obeyed. "Sit!" she said firmly.

In the small room, there were three chairs along the wall opposite her desk, and the girls sat with a chair between them. The vice principal, without losing eye contact with the girls, walked over to her chair, tossed her Blackberry onto her desk, but did not sit down. Instead, she stood with her hands on her desk and glared down at them.

A handful of blonde hair was sticking awkwardly from the left side of Kiara's head. She was sitting straight-up, doing a good job acting like nothing out of the ordinary had taken place. Misty, rubbing her throbbing ear, looked downcast and defeated. Her demeanor was in complete accord with her mussed-up brown hair. She had felt the wrath of Mrs. Francis on two other occasions. She wished she were facing Principal Christianson.

In one smooth move, Mrs. Francis, with her firm, powerful eyes fixed squarely on the girls, leaned forward and placed one hand flat on the desk to brace herself. "Now . . . let's see." She hesitated as she tapped her cheek with her index finger. Each word in her next sentence was enunciated one after another in a slow, even flow. "You two are third graders, am I correct?"

The girls, bitten by the derision, looked away in silence.

"RIGHT?" Mrs. Francis roared, and both girls jumped. She paused and searched their faces for signs she now had the upper hand.

Misty knew Mrs. Francis did not like her. The last time she was sitting in this chair was for slamming Melissa Stanford against the wall for flipping her the bird, and the vice principal had outright told her that she thought Misty was the boldest, in-your-face student she had ever had to deal with. Now, Misty was beaten down, for the moment at least, nothing more than a wilted lily. Kiara, on the other hand, continued to sit up straight and act like nothing was wrong.

Mrs. Francis stared angrily at the girls. She lowered her voice and said firmly, "Fighting solves nothing, do you hear me? It's not what we do in this school. This little brawl you two engaged in is a disgrace to your parents, your classmates, and to Wabaunsee Valley."

After a long pause, Mrs. Francis sat down. "Okay, girls, what's the story here? Kiara, we'll start with you."

Kiara cleared her throat and began in a casual tone, "Like . . . me and Misty were just horsin' 'round a bit, and somehow it just got to be somethin' wild." She turned and looked at Misty. "Ain't that right, Misty?"

"What?" Misty howled. She had refused to narc on Kiara for lesser evils, but she wasn't going to let her nemesis get away with such a painful and unjustified attack. "I was just comin' outta the bathroom"—her finger pointing in Kiara's face—"and you jumped me!"

Kiara shot Misty a hate stare. "Whatever!" Then she directed her innocent eyes to the vice principal.

Mrs. Francis firmly hushed Misty, then looked at Kiara. "Everyone can see how badly you two treat each other . . . no one's going to buy that story."

"She stole my homework!" Kiara blurted out.

"I did not!" Misty countered.

"One at a time please," Mrs. Francis said firmly. "Misty, you'll get your chance to talk. Kiara, go on."

"But . . ." Misty protested.

"Quiet!" Mrs. Francis shouted. Keeping her eyes directed toward Kiara. "Explain."

"I did my math for Mr. Cobbler in study hall, got it done, and Misty did somethin' with it."

Ms. Francis cocked an eyebrow. "Misty, did you take her assignment?"

"No," Misty said firmly. "I don't have Mr. Cobbler this year. Why would I take her stupid math paper?" Deceit was a well-practiced survival tool for girls raised in abusive homes. Lies to teachers came particularly easy for Misty. When Mrs. Francis's attention shifted back to Kiara, Misty looked away and smiled.

"How do you know Misty took it?" Mrs. Francis asked. "Did you see her take it?"

"I didn't see her, but Laura said she took it."

"Okay, did Laura see her take it?"

Kiara leaned forward. "Laura said she saw Misty go by my desk while I talked to Mr. Simpson." All three girls were in a study hall held in the Social Sciences classroom.

"Did Laura see her take it?" Mrs. Francis pressed.

"Laura said she took it." Kiara's voice became even more firm. "I know she took it!"

"Misty, what's your story?"

"I came outta the bathroom to get on my bus, and Kiara jumped me for no reason. She hurt my back and socked my ear. I had a right to hit her back!"

Mrs. Francis crossed her arms. "Did you start the fight, Kiara?"

"She took my math paper!"

"Did you attack her?" Mrs. Francis pushed.

Kiara huffed and looked away.

"I'll take your silence as a yes."

Mrs. Francis stood and moved to the front of her desk, then sat on top of it. "Listen," she said in a kind voice, "you are both intelligent girls. You should focus on your schoolwork. Ignore each other. You can be better than what you are, can be happier than what you're making yourselves now. The way you're treating each other can't be getting you what you want from school."

The girls stared at the floor. They remained silent as the vice principal lectured them. Misty wanted to cry, but not because of Mrs. Francis's words, nor because of the bad blood between she and Kiara—it was just stressful, and she wanted it to be done with.

Mrs. Francis stood and looked down at the girls. In the solid, steel voice all too familiar to misbehaving students, she concluded the matter. "This kind of behavior is unacceptable here. You are both suspended from school for the next five school days."

"Me?" Misty exclaimed. "Why me? I didn't do nothin' but fight her back!"

"The teachers said both of you were hitting at each other, and I would appreciate it if you did not interrupt. You are both suspended for five days. When you return to school, you both will be talking to a social worker. If anything close to this happens again, the punishment will be much worse. I sincerely hope each of you will do some soul searching about how you can resolve your differences and put a stop to this kind of behavior."

Misty again protested, "You just wait till my mom finds out I did nothin' wrong—"

"Your mom is already here," Mrs. Francis snapped. She's waiting in the office. You are free to go, Misty, and I hope to see a different young lady when you return to school a week from tomorrow."

Misty followed Mrs. Francis out the door and into the outer office. Her heart pounded. Her mother Phyllis

Wendell, was not someone to anger. *Mom is gonna be so pissed,* she thought.

But as Misty entered the room and saw her mother standing there, she knew something was wrong. Her mother had quite the reputation for being volatile, but the feisty mom wasn't there to defend her. Misty's puzzled eyes searched her mom's face.

Phyllis stood silent, looked away, remained expressionless, as Mrs. Francis briefly explained what happened and the resulting disciplinary action. Her mother's husky voice didn't offer one word in challenge when Mrs. Francis had finished. Misty was confused . . . and worried. This wasn't like her mother.

"Do you understand that Misty can't come back to school until next Wednesday?" Mrs. Francis said.

Phyllis nodded, turned to Misty, and in her raspy voice, breathed, "Let's go."

Mrs. Francis looked confused as well. "Are you all right, Ms. Wendell? Is something wrong?"

After a pause, Phyllis responded with toneless words expressing a message not at all fitting her confrontational nature. "I'm fine." She turned to Misty. "Come on, Misty, we need to go home."

The mother and daughter exited the school in silence and walked out into the cool October day. The day had begun with cold temperatures accompanied by four inches of snow. The beginning of the school day had been delayed two hours on account of the slippery roads. The temperatures had moderated quickly, and the snow was gone leaving mud and some puddles in the gravel drive.

As they approached the decade-old blue Ford, a worried Misty pleaded, "Mom, what's goin' on? You're freaking me out!"

Phyllis, struggling to hold back tears, silently motioned for Misty to get into the car. As they were putting on their seat belts, she composed herself long enough to tell her daughter that she would explain what had happened on the way home.

As they drove across the parking lot, her mother looked repeatedly up and down the highway to make sure the road was clear, then, ignoring the stop sign at the end of the school drive, turned right onto the highway.

Misty lost it. "Mom! Please!" she screamed.

Through quivering lips, her mother blurted, "Sonny's dead!"

Misty's calm response, followed by a pause, indicated her inability to accept such a message. "What?"

Her mother had to take the time to compose herself before she could speak the words again. In her gruff, angry voice, this time through tears, she said, "Sonny's dead. Someone shot him in the back of the head!"

The words plunged like a spear straight into Misty's heart. She was devastated. Had she been standing; she would have slumped to the ground in a heap. Numb, bursting with emotion, Misty could feel nothing at all. She wanted to scream but couldn't, wanted to cry but no tears would come. She felt suspended in midair, waiting for a happy landing, waiting for some word of mercy to bring her safely back to Earth.

What her mom had said wasn't possible. She had known Sonny forever. She grew up watching her older brother Chris and Sonny hang out together. They were friends. Misty was in love with him and dreamed that they would get married one day. Sonny must have known that she had feelings for him. He was always so nice to her. They smoked pot together. When her mom wasn't angry with him, Sonny still hung out at their house, sometimes for an hour or two to sit around their kitchen table, bum cigarettes, and talk. Sometimes he'd stay overnight or even for a two-or three-night stay. He wasn't dead, couldn't be!

Misty looked out at the hills and fields strewn along each side of the highway, too stunned by her mom's words to see them. The overcast sky put a dirt-brown hue to the stalks standing in the unharvested cornfields. Shredded brown stubble, with row after row of eight-inch spikes, marked those already denuded by a big red or green combine.

"Are you sure?" Misty whimpered.

Her mother had been quietly sobbing. She paused to compose herself, then howled, "Yes." She paused again, then screamed, "Yes! Yes! Dammit all to hell! He's dead! Sonny's gone and he ain't coming back!"

Misty understood the anger in her mother's voice reflected the anguish she felt over their young friend's death and had nothing to do with her. Dumfounded, she remained silent. As she watched the world go by, perceiving only what was going on inside herself, her eyes at last filled with tears.

They passed a soybean field that had retained an abundance of green. Next came a house and farm buildings with trees, one bare, others still clothed, some with green leaves, but most reflecting red, yellow, and orange, the hues dulled by the gray clouds filling the afternoon sky.

Misty had an urge to talk to Pastor Dave. They'd been friends since he moved to town six years ago. Sometimes she would go over to the church after school and they would sit together—in cold weather on the steps leading into the sanctuary, and in warm weather on the steps outside the building—and she would tell him about her day. When she missed the bus and didn't want to tell her mom, she walked to Pastor Dave's house, which was only five minutes away, and he gave her a ride to school.

34

She wanted to see Pastor Dave. It had been a few weeks since she'd seen him. She couldn't even remember why she had gotten mad at him. But now she just wanted—needed—to talk with him.

Chapter 3

The burden of snow the previous morning had brought down many of the dead leaves on the deciduous trees that lined the Little Wabaunsee River. Enough leaves remained on the branches, however, to offer an Art Nouveau portrayal of branches, darkened by the moist morning, outlining irregular splotches of yellow, orange, crimson, and bronze.

For the next few days, when the sky was clear, those fall hues would be eye-catching, vivid, full of life. On this particular Wednesday morning, such brilliance would be subdued by the gray clouds.

In the Potawatomi language, the proper name "Wabaunsee," meant "leader." Early pioneers named the river in honor of the Native American chief whose tribe was encamped near its banks. Over time, the adjective "little" was attached because of the waterway's small size.

Moving north up Route 99, an eighteen-wheel grain truck approached the line of fall color along the river. The roar of the truck's powerful engine, accompanied by the whining of its wheels, had betrayed its presence to the ears of those north of the watercourse before the large truck appeared. Carrying a load of the Midwest's golden corn, the huge vehicle rounded a curve and burst into sight as it passed over the bridge.

Continuing through the fertile flood plain on the other side of the river, the driver downshifted for the climb to the top of the bluff. As the rig reached the crest of the hill, it had officially entered the town of Baunsee, a sleepy, little place now abuzz with talk of a murder, the first in its 134-year history.

Vehicles entering Baunsee from the south got the best visual impression of the village.

Halfway up the hill a treeless pasture to the right contained small goats, which added interest for passersby. Farmhouses and outbuildings dotted the hill just below the outdated but well-cared-for sign that read: "Baunsee, population 384." Inside the village limits, Route 99, South Main Street, featured newer and better-kept homes and lawns.

Not only did the older, run-down houses on North Main lack esthetic appeal, but power-lines, decorated with a tangle of wires and transformers, were next to the roadway. Travelers using 99 to go south would not see much as they entered the village of Baunsee. The view of a beautiful rock garden, waterfall, and well-kept fishpond were obstructed by tall bushes.

The town's business district—or what was left of it—featured a boulevard in the center of a broad street. It offered sufficient parking for truckers who wanted to stop and eat at Shelly's Place, a quaint restaurant with a reputation for tasty home-cooked food and the latest gossip.

Across the street from the restaurant was a prosperous new quick shop the townspeople referred to as the "gas station." The church where Dave pastored was across the alley from the gas station. Two white church towers—one a bell tower—stretched upward toward the heavens. The new fellowship hall occupied the space behind the majestic old building.

The only building in town with a feature standing the height of the church spires was a turn-of-the-century three-story red brick school building which had a mediaeval turret. The Cone Spire Roof was taller even than the surrounding trees. The building, abandoned in 1973, was affectionately remembered by the townsfolk who had been taught there. Over the last decade, the abandoned building had been purchased in secret by a wealthy family from the east who repaired and remodeled the interior of the north end of the building. Without explanation, the school grounds had been left to Mother Nature.

At first the citizens of Baunsee were grateful someone was doing something with the "haunted school," as the children called it. Their appreciation was quickly ended by a drug bust, trial, and lengthy prison sentence for one of the wealthy family's college-educated children.

This was the town Pastor Dave ministered to, had grown to love, and served with pleasure. And since yesterday morning, the town was in whispers about the death of Sonny James Wigg.

* * *

Pastor Dave, always in a hurry, quickened his pace up the walkway toward a side door of the historic church building. Wearing khakis, a blue-checkered cotton shirt, brown shoes, and a dark blue jacket, he pulled the gray-wheeled case that carried his laptop into the old annex, which housed his office.

On Wednesday mornings, except holidays, members of the church were welcome to attend the "Breakfast Club," which was hosted by the church and offered coffee and donuts to all who wanted to come. It was supposed to start at eight and end at nine, but people came before eight seeking a cup of coffee. The donuts didn't arrive until after eight. It was a time for the community to convene, to chat about goings-on, all while filling their bellies with warm coffee and donuts. Today was the third meeting.

Pastor Dave attended these "meetings," but he never made it until after eight. Today he was even later. The traumatic conclusion of yesterday's walk, and its aftermath, had left him tossing and turning throughout the night, unable to sleep until the wee hours of the morning.

His office was down a hall to the right. To his left was a twelve-foot opening into the century-old sanctuary. The pleasing odor of the old building was accompanied by a tasteful mauve carpet, dark-stained wooden pews, and two rows of milk-glass light fixtures suspended on chains. Stained-glass windows gave the room light, color, grace, and sanctity.

After a brief stop in his office, Pastor Dave entered the new fellowship hall. There were a dozen people, mostly women, including Jenny, the part-time church secretary, seated on either side of a line of white resin tables. His wife, Barb, was also there—she always arrived before he did. Some had brought their own coffee mugs—a variety of shapes, sizes, and colors—while others sipped from white styrene cups. The men were wolfing down donuts or delicious, warm cinnamon rolls fresh from Beulah's oven. Beulah, a devoted church member for decades, was an excellent cook, and paradoxically, as skinny as a rail.

What Dave heard upon entering the room seized his attention, preempting the normal cheery greeting offered to each one present. Raymond Elders, a former member of the ambulance crew had the floor. He was tall, of medium build, retirement age but not retired, and an obnoxious know-it-all.

"Ya know what I mean?" his gruff voice barked. "I mean, it kinda makes ya think: wa' did the ga-damn kid get hisself into? Ya know what I'm a-tellin' ya? To do w'at they did to 'em . . ."

Tim abruptly stood and charged toward the exit. He didn't often darken the door of the church and was not a particularly religious man, yet he was known around town for his judgmental attitudes. Tim and Ray didn't care much for one another. On his way to the exit, he breezed by Pastor Dave, who was just returning his wallet to his back pocket after making a donation.

Three meetings of the Breakfast Club, and three times Ray had found a way to push Tim's buttons, getting the exact reaction everyone thought he desired. On the other hand, this thrice-repeated drama resulted in no reaction at all on the part of the others present, not even Tim's wife, Mary Lou, who took a sip of coffee as she remained seated.

Ray continued as though nothing had happened. "I don't wanna judge nobody or nothin', ya get my drift? But I was told by somebody in a position ta know that the kid's hands were missin'! If his hands are missin', then they got somethin' what didn't belong to 'em, if ya' know what I'm sayin'."

There was a long pause. Dave, who was now standing at the kitchen serving window, turned around to face the group. He was holding a plastic cup full of coffee and a small paper plate with two cake donuts. He started toward a vacant folding chair along the men's end of the table.

As the self-appointed defender of the community's down-and-outers, he couldn't let this rumor go unchallenged. Dave prided himself in not being judgmental toward the less fortunate. It was a delusion, of course. He was as prejudiced as he could be toward those who looked down on others they considered below them. In terms of illicit pride, there was no difference at all between himself and the critics he criticized.

Dave's soft-spoken voice had an edge. "So, Ray, you heard Sonny was killed by drug dealers 'cause he was holdin' out on 'em? And then they cut off his hands to send a message?" As he spoke, he noticed a few of the women grimace. Barb glared at him.

Ray backed off a bit. "I wasn't there, and I don' know, ya know what I'm sayin'? That's what I heard. They shot 'im in the back o' the head and cut off 'is hands." He pointed at Dave and said, "And they can't find Tina neither!"

Dave placed his coffee, donuts, and two napkins—he always took two napkins—on the table and sat down in the metal chair. He grimaced as a sharp pain in his knee caught him up short. There wasn't much of a bruise on his knee, but it hurt like crazy when he bent it. Dave placed his hands on the table to steady himself. The room was silent as they watched him.

Having made his point, and not wanting to create more tension, Dave made no further comment. He had no intention of letting anyone know he had found Sonny or had any firsthand knowledge about the matter.

He took a sip of coffee, then bit into the donut. All eyes were still on him. He ignored their stares and mulled over what Ryan had said. Sonny's hands were in tact when Dave found him yesterday morning. That was a fact. The boy being shot in the back of the head, on the other hand, seemed plausible . . . but wouldn't there have to be an exit wound somewhere around his face? Dave had seen none. Besides, Sonny still had enough life in him to cry out. And that last garbled outcry . . . *what on earth was that all about? Sounded almost like he was trying to tell me something?* Dave thought.

During the awkward silence, Jenny stood, smiled, took her coffee, and left the room, presumably to begin her morning work. She was scheduled to be at the church three days a week from nine to noon. In reality, there was a good deal of flexibility to both her hours and days, but she always got her work done.

Al, the congregation's resident comedian, attempted to break the uncomfortable hush in the room with a joke. It fell flat. The talk then zeroed in on the climate and how it was different than it used to be. Dave tuned everything out as he ate his donuts and drank coffee, catching snippets about unseasonable snows along the way. The image of Sonny haunted him. Not to mention the sound of his scream echoing in the dawn. And now he couldn't help but worry about Tina. Perhaps Tina had been abducted as Ray had implied.

Suddenly, Jenny appeared at the door and motioned for Dave. He got up and went to the door. There's a phone call for you . . . Penelope Timkin," she said when they were far enough down the hall so no one could hear them.

Penelope was Sonny Wigg's maternal grandmother.

In his office, Dave closed the door, and, cautious about his sore knee, sat down, picked up the receiver, and said, "Penelope?" He heard the click as Jenny hung up her phone. "I am so, so sorry to hear about Sonny. What can I do for you, how can I help you?"

Penelope's voice, husky from years of smoking, struggled to answer. "Can you . . . can you do . . . the funeral?"

"Yes, yes, certainly," Dave answered, ignoring the shaken woman's strange way of beginning the conversation. "I would be glad to do the services for your family, but do you need me now? Would you like me to come over to talk with you and Larry?"

"Not now," she answered. "Tina . . ." She broke down in tears. It took some time for her to pull herself together again. "She's comin' back from Arkansas and'll be here sometime this mornin'. We told her not to go to her house, but to come here . . . to come straight to our house. She doesn't know yet, and we wanna tell her. She'll want you ta do the service." The woman was sobbing.

It made sense to Dave that Tina didn't know about her son's death. She was out of town and unreachable, and the police had to inform whatever family members they could find.

"Are you sure you don't want me to come over and be there when she arrives?"

"No, she'll be scared if she sees you here."

Tina's only contact with Pastor Dave had been when her daughter was killed. Her parents wanted to tell her of Sonny's death, and he needed to respect that. "Let me give you my cell phone number," he said.

He waited for her to get something to write on, then told her his number and asked her to repeat it back. They said their goodbyes and hung up.

Dave's heart felt heavy. "What a crappy mess this is," he said to the empty room. He started to pop up out of his office chair but pain stabbed him in the knee. "Shit!" he exclaimed, as he plopped back down. He sat there for a moment rubbing his knee. It didn't hurt when he didn't move it.

Someone tapped on the office door. "Come in," Dave called out. He heard his perpetually upbeat wife say something to Jenny across the hall.

"My hands are full, open the door for me," Barb called through the door.

Dave stood up—slowly this time—and opened the door.

Barb stood there with a donut in one hand, a fresh cup of coffee for him in the other, and a newspaper clenched under her left elbow. "We're cleanin' up," she said, as she closed the office door. "They're leavin'."

Dave looked at the clock. "Didn't realize it was this late," he said, as he put the coffee and unfinished donut on his desk. "Thank you."

Barb handed him the newspaper. "You'll want to see this."

Dave took the newspaper. "That was Penelope on the phone. They're waiting for Tina to get home. She's been in Arkansas," he said.

The newspaper had been folded so one of the central columns was exposed, and a small article was circled with blue ink. He quickly read the brief article:

46

BAUNSEE MAN DEAD

Early yesterday morning, a Baunsee man was found unconscious in his yard. The man, whose name is not being released pending notification of next of kin, was pronounced dead at Mercy Hospital in Gillespie.

The Potawatomi County Sheriff's office is releasing few details, but the investigating officer said foul play was suspected.

"Are you going over to see Penelope?" Barb asked.

"I offered, but they didn't want me to come over yet. Penelope asked me to do Sonny's funeral, but she said Tina doesn't even know Sonny's dead yet."

"Awful!" Barb said with concern written in her eyes. She shook her head. "You get too involved in situations like this." Differences of opinion aside, Dave knew his wife cared deeply about him and hurt right along with him when he was distressed.

"It'll be okay. I'll be staying in town today, so I'll be home for lunch . . . unless they call, of course." He reached out and pulled Barb toward him. They gave each other a warm hug. Barb's hug was extra tight, full of acceptance and understanding.

"Was he shot?"

Dave shrugged. "Like I told ya, there was blood all over the back of his head. I don't know. His hands were not cut off, that I do know."

"Tragic," Barb answered. "Even though..." She paused, glancing at his face "He was what he was." Dave was all too familiar with his wife's low opinion of struggling young people who failed to live up to polite societal expectations. He was glad she chose to stop herself from making a comment about Sonny that he would have felt compelled to respond to.

"See you at home," Barb said in a serious tone. She closed the door behind her.

His wife was a worrier, many of her fears about small stuff. Now she had a concern about him that he thought to be justified. He just happened to be there to find Sonny. Why him? He would never forget the moment it got light enough to see the blood—and that scream, that last haunting scream. He shivered.

* * *

About an hour after Barb left, Dave stepped out of his office and across the hall to give Jenny information for the Sunday morning bulletin. He heard a noise coming from the sanctuary. Neither he nor Jenny were surprised, as it was not uncommon for a member of the congregation, or someone from the community, to go into the sanctuary to think or pray without announcing their presence. He concluded his business with the secretary and quietly peeked into the sanctuary to determine if he could be of service.

Misty!

She was sitting in one of the pews with her head in her hands. He was not surprised to find her here, nor at the fact that Phyllis had allowed the girl to stay home from school. He knew she and Sonny were friends, and she would be upset, terribly upset. Misty's attendance at church was sporadic, and he hadn't seen her for a couple of months.

As he walked up the aisle, he cleared his throat to let her know he was approaching. Misty looked up, saw him, cried out as she jumped to her feet, slid from between the pews, threw her arms around him, and sobbed. Many times, Misty had played the role of a drama queen. But these tears, this sorrow, was a genuine reflection of a heart-rending personal loss.

Her arms encircled his chest, and without saying a word, he put his arms around her with one hand behind her head. "I know, I know . . . you lost a good friend and it hurts." He caught a faint whiff of perfume.

"It hurts so bad . . . it hurts so bad . . . I can't stand it . . . I just can't stand it!" she cried out.

They stood there holding each other for some time. Misty, trembling, comforted in her pastor's arms, alternated between quiet tears and loud sobs.

After a time, Dave gently grabbed Misty's shoulders and broke away. "Let's sit down and talk," he said. He was worried about someone coming into the church building and seeing him with his arms around a fourteen-year-old girl. Misty's face was wet and her nose was running. She dabbed her leaking nose with a tissue too soaked to be of any use.

"You sit, I'll get more Kleenex," he said, and then retrieved a box of tissues from the front pew. When he returned she was seated, her face buried in her hands. He put the box of tissues beside her and then sat down. She threw the old tissue on the pew and then pulled out three new ones. As she mopped up her tears and blew her nose, she gulped a quick series of breaths in the reflexive manner of one in the midst of a good cry.

"They killed him, Pastor Dave! They murdered him!" Her voice was full of emotion: tight, angry, brittle. "They shot him in the head and cut off his hands!"

Dave put his arm on the back of the pew behind her and gently rubbed her shoulder.

Jenny peeked into the sanctuary. He nodded. She left without saying a word as he continued. "I'm so sorry for you and your family," Dave said.

"I know who done it too! I know who murdered him and why, Pastor Dave! It's wrong, it's evil! I hate 'em!"

Startled, Dave paused. "You know who did this?" He paused again. "Have you said anything to the police?" Misty didn't answer. After a fourth pause, Dave asked, "If you do know something, Misty, you need to tell the police."

Misty buried her head in Dave's shoulder and started to cry again. The sobs came out in trembling bursts. When her crying subsided, she took more tissues and wiped her raw nose.

"Tell me about Sonny," Dave said. "You knew him well. Tell me about the Sonny you knew."

Misty stared into the distance. Her eyes were glossy. Then the words came pouring out, often with tears, but a couple of times with laughter about ways Sonny had amused her.

Her family had moved to Baunsee when she was seven, and she had met Sonny soon after. She described Sonny's friendship with her older brother, Chris, and how they had hung out together, how Sonny would come over and play with her and her brother, and he teased her when she was younger. She told him how he had taught her to smoke. Last week he'd come over to their house, as he often had in recent years, to mooch smokes from her mom, talk, and stay overnight.

Misty poured out her heart, then, without warning, her countenance transformed. From a vulnerable fourteen-year-old girl spilling out overwhelming grief and sorrow, she morphed into a vengeful, rage-filled she-devil. She sat upright in the pew, became rigid, and her voice deepened. "If I could get a gun," she said, "I'd kill 'em myself!"

Dave studied Misty's fire-filled eyes. He had never seen her this upset. In all fairness, he didn't for one minute believe she could, or would, shoot someone, but she had such a bold nature, so in-your-face when she was upset, and there was more than ample reason to think she might do something to put herself in danger or get her in trouble. He was shaken by her whole demeanor.

"Kill who?"

"The ones who killed Sonny!" she answered. "I know who done it, Pastor Dave, I swear I know who done it!"

"Then you need to tell the police, Misty. Promise me you won't do something foolish."

"The cops won't do nothin' 'cause Greg hates Sonny!"

Dave needed to calm her down. "If you have evidence, Misty," he said in a soft voice, "you need to give it to the police. They are more than capable of dealing with this. They will—"

His cell phone rang, causing him to jump. He pulled the phone from his pocket and looked at the small screen. "I've got to take this call." He looked Misty in the eye, his voice intense, "Promise me you won't do anything stupid, Misty, please. I've got to take this call."

Misty looked away.

"Misty, promise me!"

The phone rang.

There was a pause. The phone rang a fourth time.

"I won't try to kill nobody, I promise."

Dave got up and walked out of the sanctuary. He quickly answered. "Hi, Penelope. Hang on a minute," he said. He hurried to his office and shut the door behind him.

"Hi, Penelope," he said again.

"Tina's here, please come. We need you!" Penelope's gruff voice was full of fear. Her words were heavy, effectively communicating her angst for her beloved daughter.

Dave clenched his jaw. It felt as though he had failed to help Tina years ago when her daughter had been killed in a car accident. At that time she simply would not let him inside the protective wall she had built around herself. Now the stakes were even higher.

"I'll leave right now," Dave answered. He quickly hung up and gathered his things. He told Jenny he was leaving, then walked into the sanctuary, wanting further assurance from Misty that she wouldn't do anything to get herself into trouble. Misty was no longer there.

Chapter 4

Beneath a sky filled with depressing gray clouds, Dave's Ford Focus rattled as it passed over the railroad crossing on the highway just north of town, then bounced along a gravel road lined with now fallow farmland. Pushing aside the apprehension he had before most funeral consultations, he focused on the pain of the Timkin family, and on what he did best: keep his mouth shut and listen to their every word. He cared... couldn't help himself!

He turned onto a long dirt lane and followed its twisted path to a farmyard. The white wood-framed house, in need of a coat of paint, was larger than the Timkin's old home in town, where they gathered to plan their granddaughter's funeral. The home and unattached garage were in much better shape than the surrounding farm buildings. The barn had a gambrel roof that was collapsed in the middle. One of the outbuildings, no longer able to hold itself upright, had become a jumbled heap of rotting gray boards surrounded by weeds. A hog house and machine shed were well on their way to the same fate.

He parked near the gate and got out. As he closed the wire gate behind him, his attention was arrested by a sudden flurry of activity near the front door—the rapid dispersal of a bevy of cats surrounding a large cast-iron skillet with a broken handle. A small brown tabby kitten with a white front made a beeline for Dave and pressed against his leg. Penelope, her face drawn with worry, scurried out to meet him. She was wearing white sneakers, blue jeans, and a red blouse. The urgency of her movements, the look of pain on her face, and her red swollen eyes tugged at his heart.

"Penelope, this is all so tragic . . ." he began, but before he could even finish the sentence, she had thrown her arms around him.

"You've got to do somethin' for Tina!" she pleaded. "She's . . . she's . . ." The distraught Penelope buried her tear-stained face into his chest.

Over the years, Penelope had been afflicted with a number of health issues, so she looked thin and frail. But looks were deceiving. Dave knew she was a tough old bird. She had stood like a rock through a lot with Tina and other family members, one of whom was in prison.

Dave gave her as much time as she needed. He leaned his head atop hers. "I'll do what I can . . . the best I can."

She stepped back and looked at him. Mopping her eyes with a handful of tissues, she blurted, "She just won't talk!"

"What?" Dave asked.

"As soon as we told her Sonny'd been killed, she stopped talkin'. She didn't scream, won't bawl, she won't say nothin'. She won't do nothin' but sit'n smoke cigarettes!"

Dave made no verbal response as he processed Penelope's words. She then took a firm grip on his wrist and pulled him toward the front door.

Dave followed her up the three steps and onto the kitchen's ageing linoleum floor. Tina sat on the far side of the primordial 1950's green Formica kitchen table. Unkempt strands of red hair draped down over the shoulders of her blue blouse. Wearing jeans and brown loafers, her legs were crossed, and a knee supported her right elbow. Smoke from a cigarette she held between her fingers curled upward toward the ceiling.

"Tina, I'm so sorry . . ." As he approached she looked up at him. Dave would never forget the look in her eyes. Her face convulsed with pain and took on an expression so filled with hatred and contempt it stopped him dead in his tracks.

It had been Dave's intent to approach Tina, to place his hand on her shoulder as he spoke, to embrace her if she allowed it. None of those things happened. The venom her eyes hurled at him had filled him with an irrational dread, and he could do nothing but stand mute where he was.

Memories swirled in his brain, transporting him back to a moment that was permanently etched in his seven-year-old brain. He had stood in his pajamas watching his parents argue. The night before, his father had gone on another drunken rage. He cowered in the corner as he watched his mother, with a suitcase in hand, walk out the front door with the stated purpose of never coming back. He had moved to the window, pushed the curtain aside, and watched his mother walk down the sidewalk and disappear from sight. The next morning, his mom was back home. But the experience terrorized Dave, who was still living with the persistent subconscious dread of being abandoned by his mother.

And here he was, standing in the Timkin kitchen, being rejected by another mother.

Dave had made many visits to the homes of grieving families in his career. Never before had he been assaulted by a stare as venomous as Tina's. The voiceless stare of the heartbroken mother had persisted. Was it a symbolic attempt to destroy a servant of the God who had mercilessly allowed her only remaining child to be murdered?

Eyes wide, Dave looked at Penelope and then at Larry. "Should I leave? I don't want to upset—"

"No!" Their firm voices shot across the room toward him as they offered their angry daughter simultaneous scowls. With an authoritative motion of his hand, Larry motioned for Dave to sit. His own hand shaking, Dave pulled the chair out and sat across from Tina.

Dave paused for another moment to gather his emotions. He once again told them how sorry he was about Sonny. He looked at Penelope and Larry and said, "Tell me about your grandson. I want to hear about him."

For over an hour, Penelope and Larry talked while Tina smoked cigarettes, one after another. Dave listened, asked questions, sought to bring out everything they remembered about their grandchild, Sonny. It wasn't so much that Dave wanted to know, but he wanted them to talk, to engage in cleansing grief. There was an off chance it might also draw Tina out, help her feel something, see in a different way, weep, scream at God, or do anything else she needed to do to deal with the pain he knew to be locked up inside.

Penelope told stories about Sonny when he was little. There were cute stories, funny stories. One time, he'd dumped a bag of flour on the kitchen floor and made designs in it. Another time he climbed onto the kitchen table and emptied a vase of fresh flowers, then gathered them into a bouquet and offered them to his grandmother when she came in the room. When he first learned to walk, he grabbed their dog's tail and let the animal pull him faster and faster around the yard until he—in peals of laughter—fell to the ground and rolled around while the dog licked at his face. During those happy remembrances, there were plenty of tears from Penelope and even Larry.

The conversation turned to more troubling accounts of how an older Sonny had gotten himself into serious difficulties at school and around town. Larry, shoulders bent over the table, his eyes focused between Dave and the tabletop, told of the times when Sonny had been caught shoplifting both in Baunsee and Gillespie. He had been suspended from Wabaunsee Valley three times before he dropped out of school when he was sixteen. After he left school, Sonny refused to get a job, and when someone did give him work, he sabotaged himself to get the boot.

The family had caught him smoking pot and they were terrified he would continue down the same destructive path his mother had taken. They tried everything to stop him. Out of desperation, they had even asked the police one time to search the house. Nothing helped. He was smart, though; they knew he was still smoking the stuff but had never been able to find where he kept his stash.

During the entire discussion, Tina did not contribute one audible word. There were facial expressions: a discernable smile or two with earlier memories, jaw tightening later in the conversation, and once she pursed her lips and glared at her father. Those reactions aside, Tina just looked at the wall and smoked cigarettes.

At one point, Dave thought she might have been softening, but it was wishful thinking, empty hopes! She remained locked within her own internal world in some private place of her own—just Tina and the pain strangling her soul.

Other family members began to arrive. As Dave thought of just how to make his exit, he couldn't help but do so with a heavy heart. On a personal level, he continued to be unsettled by the way Tina had greeted him, but much more important, he was full of concern for what she might do to herself. His heart ached for her. She had lost everything—both of her children—and in the face of such losses, he felt like he could do nothing for her.

He prayed for the family, then Larry and Penelope sent him away with hugs. Even reserved Larry had given him a bear hug. On the way out, Dave paused on the landing just above the steps leading down to the front door. He had to say something to Tina before going. He turned and looked back across the table. She was still frozen in place.

"Do you want me to do the funeral service, Tina?" he asked.

From her paled features and clenched jaw came a crisp reply, one as direct as his question. "Yes." With unswerving eyes, she looked into his face, no smile, but certainty filling every feature. She then repeated the word with greater emphasis. Tina then looked back at the wall she had been staring at the entire visit, specifically at the wall calendar with a pretty fall picture, and took another puff on her cigarette.

Dave, lingering concern about her personal safety, was glad she would be staying with her folks. Penelope snaked her arms through his, and together they stepped down to the door where he gave her a second hug. "Keep a close eye on Tina," he whispered.

As Dave drove on to Gillespie, his mind was filled with thoughts about Penelope's extended family. He marveled at the beauty a life of hardship could conjure up in older people like Penelope and Larry. He worried about the deeply wounded Tina. And couldn't help but question the meaning of that last strange outcry Sonny made on that dreadful snowy morning. What was he trying to say? Was he trying to say anything?

* * *

Following the tense pastoral visit with the Timkin's, Dave had business in Gillespie and didn't pull back into Baunsee until four-thirty. As he came into the village, he noticed Greg in uniform sitting in his squad car—an all-white sedan—parked along Main Street in front of the old gas station. The officer parked there in an effort to deter cars and trucks from speeding through town.

Dave often pulled up next to his friend to talk about local happenings, photography, or just to shoot the breeze. Today, Dave had questions and was eager to see Greg.

The two rolled down their windows. Dave heard static from the police radio, and then the voice of a female dispatcher putting out a call. Greg was listening so Dave remained silent until the communication had ceased.

"Something you need to attend to, Greg?"

"Nah, long way from my jurisdiction."

"How's it goin'?" Dave's query, following a brief pause, was delivered through inquisitive facial features in the company of a voice inflection intended to communicate some purpose greater then cordial conversation.

"Great," Greg replied.

"Got a question for ya, Greg."

"Fire away."

"If Sonny was shot in the back of the head, how come I didn't see an exit wound for the bullet when I found him?"

"That's easy," Greg said. "Sonny wasn't shot through the head." He paused to let that sink in. "He died from blunt force trauma, a blow to the back of the head. And, to dispel another rumor . . . Tina has not been abducted, we know where she is."

"Oh!" There was a pause while Dave processed the information.

"That's not for public consumption yet," Greg continued. He had entrusted Dave with inside information before, facts Dave had kept confidential. The officer seemed to have no hesitation about sharing such things with his friend.

"That settles that," Dave replied, and then went on to tell Greg he had been asked to do Sonny's funeral and had talked to the family earlier in the day.

"Better you than me. I couldn't find anything good to say about the slippery little shit," Greg replied.

Dave was upset by Greg's reply. "He's dead now, Greg. He's no longer your concern, not a burden on society, just a flawed young man who lived a short and unfortunate life. Besides, from my perspective as a pastor, his family's feelings need to be respected."

Not wanting to irritate his well-meaning friend, Greg gave a halfhearted apology, and then made an attempt to change the subject. "Got a new camera last week, an old Leica twin lens. Now I got to see if I can find film for the blamed thing." Greg was into digital photography like everyone else, but he loved old film cameras, collected them, and liked to mess with them.

"Do they even make film for cameras anymore?"

"Yes," Greg replied, "but you won't find it in the drug stores."

They sat silent a couple of minutes, Dave still processing the information Greg had given him about Sonny's murder.

"I'd better go, it's been a long day and I'm tired," Dave said. Then he added in an apologetic tone, "Perhaps I'm a bit grouchy too."

Greg lifted his brow. "This case is gonna be closed fast. "We're going to make an arrest tonight."

Dave abruptly reversed the direction of the window he had begun to close. "Someone local? Anyone I know?"

"I doubt you've met him," Greg replied. "He's quiet, keeps to himself. It's likely you've seen him walking the streets. He's out mostly at night though. In his late teens, big sucker, red hair, always dressed in Goth, lives with his mom on the east end of town. The kids call him 'Big Red'."

"Is his first name Mike?"

Greg ignored Dave's question, a conscious omission. "He's gotten into trouble with the law just once so far as I know, a domestic thing the sheriff's office handled. Don't know much about it. I know he doesn't have a job, though, never has had."

"Think he really did it?" Dave looked into Greg's eyes.

"The evidence is circumstantial, but solid," Greg said with an air of certainty.

"Interesting." It was Dave's turn to raise an eyebrow. "I need to go, Greg, take care." Dave waved just as the officer got another dispatch.

Chapter 5

The sun shone brightly as Dave exited the church. He'd just finished leading the Thursday morning Bible study. The sun smiled down on the tiny town through a yet cloudless sky that had warmed the near-static air to pleasant levels—cool to the skin but not cold. Dave's spirits, already buoyed by a great discussion at the study, were elevated even further by the beauty surrounding him.

As his relaxed stride carried him toward the alleyway between the church and the gas station, he glanced up the street to the west. Between the old car dealership and the Harvest Moon Pub, he saw trees retaining sufficient color to garnish the clear blue sky above them.

As he approached the alley, three sparrows fluttered about, harvesting seeds from a narrow strip of grass in the alleyway. They abruptly fled. He stepped onto the Quick Shop sidewalk. Skirting the ice machine and the ironwork park bench, he reached the double glass doors and stepped inside.

The bell sounded as Dave entered. The service counter was to his left, but no one was behind it. Dave was the only customer. From the storeroom in the back a familiar voice called out, "I'll be there in a minute!" It was Gloria White, one of the part-time clerks. She was a long-time member of Dave's congregation.

Three rows of shelved merchandise extended to the right. Dave made his way to the refrigerated display cases, passing between stacks of cardboard soda boxes on the one side and a white plastic folding table on the other. Early each morning customers sat around the table sharing stories, gossip, mirth, or angst while they drink their morning coffee.

Gloria came out of the back room. Short, pleasingly plump, and typically quiet, she had an easy smile. "Thought you might come in today. How's Pastor Dave?" she said in her usual cheery voice.

"Great," Dave replied. "Any coffee left?" He knew the morning joe would likely be gone by this time.

"None left, but I'll make ya some, it won't take long."

"No worries." His eyes continued to peruse the case. "I'll find somethin' here to drink."

"Got some fresh-baked cookies in the office I'll share."

Dave looked at her and smiled. "Go ahead, Gloria, make me coffee. I need some caffeine and don't really want a soda."

He went to the table, pulled out one of the folding chairs, and sat down. The sports page was always atop the stack of newspapers by the time he arrived. The headline reflected the talk of the town, not the murder of a local "no good" but the White Sox had swept the Houston Astros to win the World Series.

"What're you doin' today?" Gloria shouted. She was at the coffee machine on the other side of the store.

"Just finished Bible study and I need to work on a funeral service when I get back to the office."

"I assume you're talkin' bout Sonny Wigg's service," she called out. "What a tragic thing. When's it gonna be?"

"Yep, it is a tragedy," Dave responded. "I don't know when it'll be. I doubt if the police have even released the body yet. All I know is the family's asked me to conduct the services." There was a pause. "I feel so badly for Tina and her parents."

"I heard they arrested somebody last night."

Just then the bell sounded and in walked an obese young man with a mess of blond hair. The man walked up to the counter. As Gloria handed him a pack of cigarettes, he asked how far it was to Gillespie, then left.

"There was nothin' 'bout it in the paper this morning. Who'd they arrest, do ya know?" Dave asked.

"I heard it was Mike Early," Gloria answered as she brought Dave a paper plate with four homemade chocolate chip cookies, "but it could be just a rumor."

"Thanks." Dave's response was paired with an appreciative smile and then a question. "I've seen a young guy walking 'round town—I think his name is Mike. Big, tall, barrel-chested, red hair, always wears black. Is that Mike Early?"

"That's him, but I'm not sure he's the one who got arrested, so don't quote me."

Dave walked over to the coffee machine, took a medium-sized Styrofoam cup and filled it with the fresh brew. He took napkins—two, no more, no less—and stood there for a few moments. His mind raced back to Tuesday morning, to Sonny—and, inevitably, that curious scream—to Tina, and the young man with red hair he sometimes saw walking the streets.

Two or three customers came and went as Dave sat at the narrow table, snacked, and drank coffee. One of the visitors was connected to his church, and all were local. Dave took a moment or two to chat with each. Business as usual.

Another customer entered, but Gloria didn't offer her usual cheery greeting. She silently took the credit card from the equally mute customer. There was an awkwardness in Gloria's voice, "Pump number three . . . Sandy?" The woman nodded.

The customer was large boned and well dressed. She wore black dress pants, and black T-strap dress shoes with two-inch heels, and a dressy white chiffon blouse.

"Sandy," Gloria asked, "have you met Pastor Dave?"

As Dave approached the woman, he remembered meeting her, although he hadn't known who she was at the time. He had gone to the Gillespie Times to purchase extra copies of an edition of the paper containing an article about the new church fellowship hall.

He noticed her nice jewelry, a chunky silver necklace with matching dangly earrings. Much more important though, he noticed her red swollen eyes. She had been crying.

"Hi, Sandy," he said, "glad to meet you." She looked toward the floor, shame flushing her face. Something was wrong.

After a brief pause, Sandy lifted her eyes, exposing her humiliation to the "holy man". The words from her mouth were hesitant, under her breath, and Dave had trouble catching what she said.

"I suppose you've heard my boy was arrested in connection with this Sonny Wigg thing." She refused to use the word "murder."

Dave's eyes widened. "I had heard," he said, his tender voice offering no further details. "I'm so sorry. Can I help you in some way?"

"I need . . . I need to talk . . . with someone." She fought back tears and looked away.

"I would be glad to talk with you, Sandy, now or at some other time, whatever is convenient."

She nodded, took her purse from the counter, and beckoned for him to follow.

As they reached the exit, Misty made a boisterous entry into the store. She was wearing jeans with ragged holes in both knees and an old gray sweatshirt.

Blast it! Dave thought. *The way news traveled in this little town, Misty must know about the arrest.*

"Hi, Pastor Dave," Misty said cheerily, gracing him with a smile. Then she saw Sandy, and her face was quickly transformed from astonishment, to pity, to possible anger.

"Hi, Misty," Dave said, smiling to his young friend as he followed Sandy out the door. *Why on earth has Phyllis allowed her to remain out of school another day,* he thought. "You take care now," he told the girl.

He quickly ushered Sandy outside. "Would you like to go to the church where we can talk in private?"

"No, I don't have time," she said.

"Well, let's sit over here." Dave gestured toward the park bench on the sidewalk a few feet away.

They sat down. Sandy sat rigid, her body facing straight forward, head awkwardly twisted toward Dave. Her hands clutched her purse, holding it tightly against herself. Dave sat on the opposite end of the bench. He felt the warmth of the sun on his hand and face as he rested his right elbow on the back of the bench between them.

Sandy paused, then began, "Last night..." The distraught woman stopped and struggled, wrestling with her emotions. For a few brief seconds, her face became contorted, her chin quivered, then, with obvious effort, she regained her composure. "Last night they arrested my boy, Michael, for Sonny's... death. I'm on my way to see him in the county jail."

"Sandy, I'm so sorry." His soft voice, filled with empathy, invited her to continue.

The wounded mother looked down, defeated, then found the strength to lift her head and gaze into his compassionate face. "The people in this town must hate us."

"No one hates you," Dave's calm voice assured. He reached over and patted her hand. "Besides," he continued, "it's just you and me here now, and I want to help you—if I can."

"Maybe he'll talk to me in jail," she said. "He never tells me anything about anything. He was gone most of Monday night, but I don't know if he was with Sonny or not. As for guns, the kid has never held a gun in his life so far as I know. John was never a hunter, and neither one of us ever thought of having a gun in our house." There was a dignity to Sandy's voice.

"Is John your husband?" Dave asked.

"Was my husband!" Sandy replied. "We've been divorced for thirteen years now. Michael and I have been on our own since he was five years old."

Just then, the bell chimed and Misty exited the shop. Dave worried about her approaching them, saying something—he didn't know what—afraid of thoughtless words adding to the burdens of the already disheartened mother sitting next to him. His fears proved unfounded. Without saying a word, Misty crossed the parking lot and onto the street heading toward her house. Dangling from her right hand was a brown plastic sack containing a half-gallon of milk.

Dave turned his attention back to Sandy. "Would you like me to call in on Michael at the jail? I've made such visits many times."

"Yes!" Sandy jumped at the offer. "I would like you to see him, and even though Michael doesn't know you—at least I don't think he knows you—I'm sure he would appreciate your support."

"I've never met Michael, but I've seen him walking around town. The question right now is if you need my support. I would be glad to meet with you when we have more time to talk."

"Thank you," she replied.

Dave took a business card and pen out of his shirt pocket, circled his cell phone number, and handed it to her. Experience told him there was somewhere around a fifty-fifty chance she would contact him again, but he needed to offer.

The distraught and bewildered woman tucked the card into a pocket of her purse and then burst into a torrent of words. Her railing embodied fear, anger, protest, and pleading. "With a gun! With a gun? How could he shoot someone with a gun when he's never shot a gun in his life? Where'd he get a gun?" She caught hold of herself. "Michael has a bad temper... I could see him getting physical, he's been in far too many fights." Her dark eyes pleaded with Dave. "But shooting someone? He wouldn't know how! How could he shoot somebody?"

Dave knew Sonny died of a blow to the back of the head, not a gunshot wound, but he couldn't tell her that. What troubled him was what Sandy said about the violent behavior her son had displayed in the past. *The poor thing will be even more frightened and upset when she's told the truth about how Sonny was killed,* he thought. He had no choice but to keep Greg's confidence.

"Do you want to make an appointment to get together and talk?" Dave asked.

"I don't know when," Sandy answered. "I've got to get a lawyer." Her hands tightened their grip on her purse and she shook her head. "Oh Lordy, Daddy's got to help me pay, I don't have it!"

"Just focus on one thing at a time," Dave suggested. "When you see Michael, why don't you see if you can talk to an officer? A deputy can help you understand just what it is you need to do and might have advice about a lawyer. When you're ready, give me a call and we can get together."

Then he took her hand, looked her straight in the eye, and said, "I can't help you with any of the legal stuff, but the church might be able to help you with finances. I do want to help you, and I'll do my best to help you get through this."

She grasped Dave's hand. "Thank you! Thank you!"

"Let me at least have a quick prayer for God to help you through this, Sandy." She consented, and after Dave's words, they both stood.

"Thank you so much, I don't feel quite so alone now." Then, voice full of honest resolve, "I will call you."

Sandy hurried off to her car, which was still parked in front of gas pump number three, and drove off.

* * *

Dave had been sitting at his desk pecking away on his laptop for the last half-hour, worrying about what he could, or should say, at Sonny's funeral. Suddenly, the old annex door flew open and banged against the wall. Dave jumped. An exuberant feminine voice calling his name accompanied the sound of quick footsteps ascending the short staircase.

In seconds, Misty was standing in his doorway and closing in on him, peppering him with words bursting from her mouth like buckshot from the barrel of a shotgun. "Oh . . . my . . . God!" she emphatically pronounced each individual monosyllable. And then, referring to Michael's mother, shot out, "What'd she say?"

Not pausing even a fraction of a second for a response, she continued, "I couldn' believe it when Mom told me this mornin' that Mike Early got busted for Sonny's murder." The young teen in her excitement was now standing right over Dave. With lightning speed, she pointed at him, her blaring words contrasting with the soft, pleasing fragrance of her perfume. "He didn't do it, Pastor Dave! I know he didn't do it, and I know who did!"

Dave was not surprised to see her, nor by her exuberance.

She stopped talking, stood up straight, and took a step back. Silent, she waited for the rebuke—more likely the dirty look she would have received for such intrusive behavior at school. Instead, Dave's mouth curled upward into a grin, and a good-natured chuckle slipped through his lips. He had a friendly and easygoing relationship with all of the teens in his congregation.

Misty leaned her shoulder against the doorframe. She then began to laugh, and for a time the two chuckled and giggled in tandem. While their antics were proceeding, Dave motioned for Misty to sit on the worn tan love seat, which had been a furnishing in the church office long before he had come on the scene.

The teen plopped her plump physique onto the forward edge of the sofa, then leaned back. Her bare knees protruded through the ragged tears in her jeans.

Dave leaned back in his chair, placing his hands behind his head, fingers interlocked. "So . . ." he said from behind smiling eyes, "Misty . . . remind me to run in the other direction the next time I see you coming at me with that look in your eye!" What Dave said didn't make a lot of sense but spun them both off into a fit of laughter.

It took a few minutes for the two to regain their composure. The north wall of Dave's office consisted of built-in bookshelves housing his personal library. As Misty peered in the direction of the theology books, her smile disappeared and was replaced with sadness.

"Sonny's dead, Pastor Dave."

"I know. I wasn't laughing about that but the rather noisy way you bounced in here and stuck your finger in my face." Disarmed, Misty smiled sheepishly, then looked away.

Dave scooted his office chair closer to Misty, leaned forward, and rested his elbows on his knees. His eyes searched the young girl's face. "Misty, you keep saying you know who did this thing. I'm concerned you'll do something foolish, something to put you in danger." The earnest warning was concluded with a plea, "Please listen to me: if you know something—if you really do know who did this—you have to tell the police."

But his concern bounced off Misty as though she was wearing a suit of armor. Hazel eyes flashing anger, she sat upright to deliver her feisty response. "Like they'd believe me! The cops never believe us when they come ta our house. They don't believe my mom, they didn't believe Chris, and they won't believe me neither."

"If they won't believe you, then talk to me and I'll tell them."

Misty's nostrils flared. "I'm gonna get proof, and then I'm goin' to the cops."

"Misty, it's too dangerous!" Dave pleaded. "Please trust me."

"I don't care!" she said dismissively. "They killed my friend, and I'm gonna make sure they pay for it." Her eyes brimmed with tears.

Dave leaned forward. "Whatever you're planning, Misty, don't do it. It's not safe. Don't open yourself up to trouble like that. I don't want to see you hurt—or worse!"

There was a pause. "Don't you know you could get yourself killed?"

Misty pursed her lips, folded her arms, and looked away. Dave made several attempts to get through to the foolish girl while she silently examined the sparkly blue polish on her fingernails. In desperation, he said, "I'm going to talk to your mom, Misty."

Misty jerked her head toward him. "You said you wouldn't tell nobody what we talked about!"

"What we talk about here is confidential, until a minor tells a pastor she's going to do something endangering herself. Your safety puts confidentiality to an end." Dave had a determined look on his face now.

"Whatever! She can't stop me neither!" She pretended to take a closer look at the polish on one of her nails.

Dave threw up his hands in a gesture of surrender. He would, in fact, talk to Phyllis, but he was not confident Misty's volatile mother could, or would, do anything to deter her headstrong daughter. The police needed to know Misty was up to something, but Dave felt compelled to speak with Phyllis first.

Seeking at least some concession, Dave said, "You're not going to do anything right away—I mean, right now—are you, Misty?"

"No," came the terse reply. "I mean . . ." The girl was thinking hard. "I don't know. I don't know!" Then, "You win, I won't do nothin'."

Though Misty had said the right words, her demeanor indicated her promise was as hollow as an old, dead log. On more than one occasion, he had experienced the clever way she could "bend" the truth and do as she pleased—like mother, like daughter. Dave also understood Misty well enough to know she would walk out if he challenged her further.

"I don't wanna talk 'bout this no more," she huffed.

In an effort to cool things down, Dave changed the subject. "By the way, how come you're not in school?"

"Got suspended," the angry girl shot back. "Got in a fight and got kicked out 'til next Wednesday." Dave opened his mouth to respond, but Misty cut him off. "Totally don't wanna talk 'bout that neither."

Dave shrugged.

"What did Mike's mom say?"

Dave shook his head. "You know I can't tell you anything about what she said."

"Yeah, like you won't tell me what Mike's mom said, but you're gonna tell my mom what I told you. That's not fair!"

Dave was quick. "Ms. Early is not a minor, and she didn't tell me she was going to do something to put herself in danger."

"Whatever!" the angry teen scowled. "I'm not gonna get killed, Pastor Dave. No one'll even know."

Dave's eyebrows lifted in alarm. "No one will know what?"

Misty must have realized that she'd said too much and clammed up again.

Frustrated, Dave changed the subject. "Do you know Michael very well?" Before talking to Greg and Sandy, Dave knew nothing about Michael but what he looked like from a distance.

"Nobody knows much 'bout Mike," Misty replied. "I only heard Sonny say he played a video game with him once a long time ago. He's got a bad temper and nobody wants ta be 'round 'im much."

"I told Michael's mother that I'd go see him in jail, so it would help me if I knew a little more about him." In one unguarded moment, Dave had made a major blunder, revealing a confidence, and at the same time creating a brand new issue between Misty and himself.

Misty perked up. "Take me with you. I want to go. Take me with you when you go see him!"

Dave wrinkled his brow. "You know I can't do that. Besides, what would be the purpose of a visit? Why would you wanna see him?"

"Well, to tell 'im I know he didn't kill Sonny." She paused. "Why're you goin' to see him?"

The question was a logical one, but Dave was still taken aback. "I'm going to show him that God cares about him and wants to be his friend no matter what he's done or what's happened to him. I'm going to show him that someone outside of his own family is thinking of him. I'm going to be a listening ear if he needs to talk. I'm going to pray for him while I'm there, and to tell him the church will pray for both him and his mother."

Dave congratulated himself on such a fine reply. Despite his deliberate omission of the hot-button issue of "confidentiality," he thought he had done an admirable job.

Misty was silent as her eyes trained on a framed print of a female Minnesota Loon and her chick hanging on the wall to the left of his desk.

"I could help Mike too. He's never been mad at me. He'd be glad to see me." She then pleaded with as much gentle feminine charm as she could muster, "Please take me with you, Pastor Dave."

"Misty, it's not my choice. The sheriff's office would never allow it. And that's the end of it."

Misty looked downcast. Dave thought about her threat to take matters into her own hands. He recalled stories he had heard about Misty's brazen behavior, standing fast against teachers, students, and her own mother in the face of perceived injustice toward herself or one of her friends.

A teacher told him an older student had gotten mad at Misty for something on one occasion, took her coat, and he and a couple of friends tried to drive out of the school parking lot with it. Misty stood in front of the car and wouldn't move. She wouldn't even flinch when the driver lurched the car forward and then slammed on the brake. The impasse ended when a teacher hurried toward them. The boys threw Misty's coat out the window and sped out of the parking lot while she retrieved it.

"I'll tell you what, Misty, if you promise you won't do whatever it is you think you're gonna do, I'll call the sheriff's office and ask if you can come with me when I go to see Michael. But that's as far as I can go." Dave was confident the sheriff's office would turn down such a request.

"Okay," Misty said after a pause. "I won't do nothin'. But you can't tell my mom anything either."

"Deal," Dave said. The agreement was ratified with a high-five.

Chapter 6

Early Monday morning, Dave draped his new navy-blue windbreaker over the bar stool in the kitchen. He filled a glass with water, then headed toward the far end of the long room encompassing their kitchen, dining area, and living room. Barb was wearing a pink terrycloth winter robe and matching slippers and was seated on the mauve flower-patterned sofa. The Gillespie Times had her full attention.

Through sleepy eyes, Dave focused for a moment on his wife's pretty face. In his eyes, she had grown more beautiful with age and gray hair. They were alone—both his children and hers were now grown and raising families of their own. Dave liked the empty nest and having Barb to himself.

Barb had done a great job of maintaining her weight and sported a calm, confident exterior, projecting what others thought to be an unflappable nature. Dave, of course, had experienced the parts of her she censored in the presence of others. He had comforted the sensitive and frightened child within. Less often, but etched more deeply into his psyche, he had withered under the assaults of an ill-served tigress.

"How was your night?" Dave's voice carried through the length of the room.

He was halfway to the davenport before Barb finished the article she was reading and replied, "Good," without looking up.

"It's not too cold this morning, so why don't you come walk with me?"

"Nope, I'm done walking outside till next summer." Her response reaffirmed an unalterable previous decision and at the same time chastised her husband for asking a question with an answer he well knew.

Dave was seated on the couch opposite Barb before it dawned on her that he was teasing. In return, she offered an over-the-top smile accompanied by words filled with exaggerated enthusiasm, "Thanks for asking though."

For the next twenty minutes, they sat in silence, as they did morning after morning, he on one end of the sofa with his nose in a news magazine and drinking ice water, and she on the opposite end reading the local newspaper and sipping hot coffee that had been—according to Dave—"corrupted" with cream and sugar.

"Oh," Barb exclaimed. "Here's something . . ." She looked up at Dave. "Did you know Michael Early is to be arraigned for Sonny Wigg's murder today?"

"Yes, yes, I did," Dave responded. Barb always got upset when he had heard something newsworthy and had not shared it with her. He hesitated before telling her, "Sandy phoned me last night during the youth meeting."

Barb looked surprised. Sandy Early? Michael's mom?"

"Yes," Dave responded.

"How'd you know her?"

"I met her in the gas station when I was having coffee. Gloria introduced me. I've been so busy I didn't think to tell you."

"When was that?"

"Last week sometime, I think Wednesday . . . nah, couldn't have been Wednesday, had to be Thursday."

"You mean you met her after Michael was arrested?"

Barb's questions, one following the other, felt more like a police interrogation than a harmless household conversation. She did this a lot, and Dave didn't like it. "Yes," he said, cutting the word short.

Barb jabbed his annoyance right back at him. "What'd she want?"

"She wants Michael to be released to her recognizance today and asked me to pray that happens." Dave looked back down at his magazine, hoping to end the discussion.

"Don't you think you should be there to support her?" Barb's suggestions were often more than suggestions.

Slightly less irritating to Dave than his wife quizzing him like some kind of law enforcement officer was Barb telling him to do something he had already planned to do. Not wanting to mar their morning's tranquility, Dave tucked his feelings. "I intend to go. She also asked me to go visit her son at the jail."

"If he's released today," Barb responded, "you can see him here in town."

Dave took a sip of his water. He looked at Barb and shook his head. "That's not gonna happen. He's charged with a serious crime—a felony—and Sandy appears to have few resources. I'm betting I'll have to go to the county jail to visit him."

Barb searched her husband's face for a moment or two, letting what he had said sink in, then, apparently satisfied with the inquest, went back to reading her paper.

Dave was not comfortable keeping things from his wife. Him not telling her about Sandy was an intentional secret, and he certainly didn't dare tell his wife that Misty Wendell had asked to go to the jail with him. His wife viewed Misty as a manipulative little feline who was a danger to his reputation. Barb had complained about him paying too much attention to her, and his carelessness about when and where the two kept company. He was often looking after the troubled teens in the church's he served.

Making Dave even more uncomfortable was the fact he had phoned the sheriff's office last Friday to ask if he could bring Misty along when he made a pastoral call on Michael. The officer he'd spoken with on the phone had given a negative answer but added that he would pass the request along. Even the possibility, no matter how small, that he and Misty would ride in the same car to Gillespie would send Barb through the roof.

He felt caught between the insecurity compelling him to be more open with his wife than was wise—a character flaw which had gotten him into trouble more than once—and the proper professional ethics of keeping Misty's petition confidential.

Dave swallowed the rest of his water. He knew Barb sensed he was hiding something from her. This fear—real or imagined—compelled him to hasten his departure from the house. He took the empty glass to the kitchen sink, retrieved his outerwear, and as he passed in front of Barb on his way to the front door, he leaned over to give her a peck on the lips. He felt Barb's eyes burning a hole in his back as he closed the door behind him.

* * *

In full escape mode, Dave left the circle of light offered by a streetlamp and entered the welcoming darkness that enveloped his beloved pre-dawn world of Baunsee, Illinois.

His morning walks were so important to his mental health. Outside he could feel the exhilaration, the release, the safety of God's wonderful world, and there sort through his own place within it.

This was his selfish time. He cared about his people, especially the wounded ones. It was difficult for him to watch others do what he did to himself when he was younger: reject the help from those who were in a position to help and who wanted nothing more than to aid him.

His thoughts turned to Sonny's funeral. It had been a private family affair, held Saturday at the Jessup Memorial Gardens in Gillespie. Dave recalled the faces of some of the family members, but he remembered few of their names.

For most funerals that Dave officiated, he sensed the deep feelings of hurt within the surrounding friends and family. Occasionally, a family member's emotions were being governed by something else, some kind of deep-seated anger either toward the deceased or for what had happened to the deceased.

Among those who had gathered for Sonny's funeral service, anger seemed to be the predominant emotion, in particular among the younger men. They fed each other's ire prior to the funeral service, which resulted in a toxic atmosphere that troubled both Dave and Franklin Jessup, the senior partner in the firm who owned and operated Jessup Memorial Gardens in Gillespie.

Of even greater concern to Dave was the effect this atmosphere seemed to have on Misty. In the twenty minutes between the warm hugs with which Misty and Phyllis had greeted Dave, to the time the funeral director urged the mourners to be seated in the chapel prior to the family's entrance for the service, Misty had spoken to three younger male relatives of Sonny and, from her facial expressions, it appeared to him she was being caught up in their animus. This, of course, had revived Dave's worries about Misty doing something to put herself at risk.

Sonny's grandparents, Larry and Penelope, didn't have a vindictive bone in their bodies. Whatever their struggles had been in their younger years, they were sweet, loving people despite being uneducated, poor, and burdened with an overabundance of life's miseries. Their mannerisms and expressions at the funeral communicated only sadness, hurt, and loss. They sought out Dave for comfort, solace, and warm hugs—not so much the hugs for Larry.

Tina did what she was supposed to do: enter the chapel and lead her family in, and sit in the front row. But never once did she look at Dave during the service. With one notable exception, the traumatized woman uttered no sound before, during, or following Dave's best efforts to bring her the consolation she couldn't, and wouldn't, accept.

After the benediction, Dave stood before the casket, ready to offer comfort to any who took the opportunity to file by the coffin for a final gesture of farewell. Tina, Penelope, and Larry remained in their seats while the few close friends and other relatives accepted the director's invitation to take a final look at their silent companion and kinsman.

The older relatives, as well as the younger women, wept. It had been hard for Dave to read the agonized expressions on the faces of the younger males as anything but the result of a thirst for revenge on behalf of their slain relative. One of the teen boys smiled from ear to ear in inappropriate affect.

At last, Penelope and Larry had approached the coffin and wept as they stared at their lifeless grandson. Dave stood behind them and put a hand on their shoulders to lend silent pastoral comfort and strength.

After saying their goodbyes, Larry left Penelope before the coffin and walked over to Tina, who was still sitting. He took her hand, giving it a gentle tug.

"No," she had softly pleaded. "I can't," she whispered.

"Ya gotta say goodbye, ya just gotta," Larry urged. He refused to release his daughter's hand, which resulted in a stalemate that lasted a full minute. Penelope, full of her own grief, was unable to separate herself from her grandson's coffin. She blew her nose into a wad of tissues and continued to weep.

At last Tina got up—slow, unsteady, depending upon her father's strength. Larry had then nudged the grieving daughter and shattered mother the arduous few steps to the casket. He was determined to provide whatever might his wounded daughter would need to take one final look at her beloved son.

Dave stepped to the side. Penelope reached out, and Tina clutched her hand as her father extended his arm across her back. Tina stood there, fixing her eyes on a blue carnation a mourner had placed on her son's white shirt.

Dave would never forget the moment when Tina looked into the inert face of her once-animated son and truly felt the excruciating pain of this massive loss piled atop so many others. She screamed. Gripped by overwhelming emotion, she had torn herself away from her startled parents and threw her arms around Dave, burying her red hair in his chest. She sobbed, letting herself wail with no inhibition, no reservation, no shame.

At first, the heartbroken mother accepted the warmth of one associated with the God who, without warning, without justification, had swept her son away from her. That changed, though, the transformation sudden and decisive. Tina froze, grew silent, stiffened, then shoved Dave away. She sneered at him, loathed him. His God had done this! Dave had wanted to help the boy's family, and he had given it his best shot, but with the exception of Penelope and

Larry, he was unsure he had contributed anything of value to anyone else.

A sadness filled him, and he tried to shake it off. He had enjoyed his morning walk, but thoughts of Tina and Sonny and Misty—at times it could be a bit much to handle. Dave crossed his driveway and bounded up the cement steps to the front door.

* * *

Jaw muscles taut with frustration, Dave braked to allow the Toyota Yaris the space it needed to exit the parking spot. When he arrived at the courthouse a few moments ago, the parking lot was full, and this was his second trip around the block in search of street parking. He pulled his car into the empty space. It was 10:40 a.m., ten minutes after the Circuit Court secretary had told him the legal procedures for the day were scheduled to begin.

As the exasperated pastor exited his car, he recalled the driver of the Yaris—a young woman who was a student at the new community college located just south of the courthouse. He now empathized with those who blamed the influx of students for the shortage of area parking.

On his way to the main entrance, located in a newer gray-block addition on the south side of the beautiful mid-eighteenth-century Romanesque Revival courthouse, Dave was grateful for the day's above-average temperatures. He passed to the left of a massive oak tree in the square, its distinctive acorns and yellow leaves littering the ground.

Once inside the building, Dave placed his belt, car keys, and loose change into a plastic container, then sent it along with his windbreaker through the X-ray machine while stepping through the metal detector. Hurrying up the steps, vaulting the lower ones two at a time, Dave made a sharp right turn at the top and proceeded down the hall toward a set of double doors.

Unsure of himself in the unfamiliar setting, Dave paused before the doors. Peeking through one of the narrow windows, he saw the black-robed judge—a distinguished-looking Caucasian man—seated behind the elevated bench.

Two people crossed the courtroom from the left and stood before the judge. On the left was a tall, thin man wearing a gray tweed sports coat. To the man's right, dwarfed by her counsel, stood a slim middle-aged woman in gray slacks and a chiffon blouse. The woman's every move communicated unease.

Dave caught sight of Sandy sitting to the right of an elderly man and woman in the visitors' gallery. He slipped into the room intending to sit in the mostly empty pew just behind Sandy, but she spotted him and waved him over. "Thank you," she mouthed, happy that he'd made it.

The judge reviewed the indictment on his desk, then lifted his head and looked at the woman standing before him. "Christine Hudson?"

"Yes," she confirmed, strain evident even in the one-word response.

The bailiff was standing at a Secretary Desk to the far left. The court clerk and court recorder sat in boxes on either side of the judge. Seated at the prosecutor's table was a young blonde-haired woman dressed in a gray suit. Three other men were seated just inside the bar.

As Dave surveyed the room, he heard the judge explain the charges against the woman, tell her the consequences if found guilty, and heard her lawyer offer a plea of "not guilty." In what struck Dave as an unbelievably short time, the arraignment was over. The woman and her towering lawyer stepped out of the bar and left the courtroom.

Sandy took a moment to introduce Dave to her parents. The Carlyles, Frances and Ralph, lived in Fayette, Illinois, a couple of hours from Baunsee. Dave smiled and shook Ralph's hand, at the same time nodding politely to Frances. Both returned Dave's smile, but Ralph, seated to his daughter's left, continued to clutch his hand as he quietly expressed his appreciation for Dave's presence.

Three court actions followed, two of them arraignments, lasting only a few minutes each, and the third was a sentencing hearing for someone who had already been convicted for a drug offense of some kind.

Dave was impressed with the way the adjudicator, following the arguments in the sentencing hearing, turned his attention to his task. Beads of sweat appeared on the judge's brow as he audibly wrestled with the issues of justice, carefully looking through papers, and weighing options before pronouncing the sentence.

While the convicted, and now sentenced man was led away by the officers, Dave turned to Sandy and asked if she had been given a specific time for Michael's arraignment. But before she could answer, the mention of Michael's name—not an announcement, but couched in instructions from the judge to other court officials—riveted the attention of the courtroom.

Wearing an orange jumpsuit and shackled at the wrists and ankles, Michael shuffled into the room with a deputy on either side. The left side of his face and left eye were badly bruised. The whole time he was looking at his mother until he was forced to turn and face the judge. Sandy offered a pitiful moan. She squeezed her parents' hands so hard her knuckles turned white. Both of the legal practitioners who had been sitting in the jury box joined Michael as the officers brought him before the judge.

Dave was shocked at the sight of Michael's bruised face. "What on earth?" His voice was loud enough to attract a glare from the bailiff.

"He got in a fight with another prisoner," Sandy whispered.

Dave was suspicious.

"Michael, told me," Sandy's voice quivered.

The judge affirmed the name of the accused, and then read the case number and charge: "The people of the state of Illinois verses Michael Franklin Early for the second degree murder of Sonny James Wigg."

The not-guilty plea offered by one of the lawyers—a nice looking youth who seemed much too young to Dave—was predictable, as was the acceptance of the trial date offered by the judge. The request for Michael to be released to his mother's recognizance, however, was a far different matter.

The attorney for the state—a practiced orator, animated, and well prepared—tipped the scales immediately. Michael had a history of violent temper outbursts. His high school career ended in the middle of his junior year after he hurled his thirty-pound backpack at a female teacher who was struck in the shoulder by the missile. The defendant's violent outbursts, the prosecutor pointed out, were pertinent to the issue at hand because neighbors had offered testimony about loud quarrels between the defendant and his mother, and on one occasion, a sheriff's deputy had been summoned to the Early home by neighbors because of a noisy altercation.

Dave felt uneasy when he realized what Sandy and Michael were up against. Sandy looked shell-shocked. Realizing how hard she had been squeezing her parents' hands, she let go.

The clincher in the prosecution's argument against Michael's release was yet to come. Michael was a loner, few, if any, friends in Baunsee, but through recent years he had spent much of his time playing online computer games with a variety of people in several different states as well as in Canada. With no friends to hold Michael in Baunsee, combined with a troubled relationship with his mother, any of those he played his games with would offer a tempting place for Michael to flee and hide from the law.

The prosecutor's assertions were devastating, countering the lame but only available argument for the defense: Michael's computer, and ability to become involved in online gaming again, would keep him at his home until his trial.

At some point while observing the arraignment and custody hearing, Dave had noticed Chris was one of the sheriff's officers holding the prisoner in custody. He thought nothing about it until after he had left Sandy and her parents in the hallway outside the courtroom—the goodbye had been a quick one, as the Early family had a meeting with Michael's lawyers.

"Pastor Dave!" Dave was down the hall and at the top of the stairs, about to descend, when he heard Chris's voice. The officer was hurrying up the hall toward him.

"Hi, how ya doin'?" Dave smiled broadly, and they clasped hands.

"Sorry, Pastor Dave, don't have a lotta time to talk. But the sheriff wants ta see ya. Can ya drop by his office?" And then, without waiting for a reply, "It would be good if ya could see him today." The deputy offered no further information and left before Dave could respond with anything but a quick nod.

As Dave began his descent to the first floor, he mulled over why the sheriff would want to meet with him. Did this meeting have to do with Misty? Would he really allow her to visit Michael?

"We probably wouldn't have purchased this old building if Noah hadn't fallen in love with the tower."

Chapter 7

It was just after one in the morning on Tuesday, overcast, and with strong gusts of wind periodically churning the darkness concealing the slumbering little village. The combination of inky blackness and boisterous winds made the perfect night for cats on the prowl, cat burglars, and vengeful agents on a mission of enmity. Standing in the shadows just outside of a fence that caged two mangy dogs was a lone figure in dark clothing concealed in the night.

The two mixed-breed mutts—the larger one mostly black Lab, the other the size and coloring of a rat terrier—were standing on hind legs, front paws braced on the fence wire. The purpose of the ghostlike figure was to keep the dogs content and silent.

The black shape offered generous strokes, scratches, and pats, then abandoned the satisfied hounds and silently moved to a back corner of the home to which the small dog pen was attached. Keeping low, one knee to the ground, the black-clad figure placed a steadying hand against the ancient white asbestos siding. The nervous but determined figure waited and watched, eyes straining in the darkness to survey the terrain between the house and back fence. A thick layer of dry leaves covered much of the back lawn.

The motionless avenger waited with uncharacteristic patience. On nature's own schedule, a strong gust of wind approached. Remaining low, but rising enough to lift a knee from the earth, the black silhouette was ready to spring. The stiff breeze tossed the leaves in the backyard into a whirlwind.

By the time the gust of wind was spent and the leaves had begun to settle back to earth, the place at the back corner of the house had been vacated. The figure was now beyond the back fence, moving swiftly along the fence line through the ryegrass and clover.

Making her way two hundred yards through the pasture, the avenger sprawled her breathless, out-of-condition body belly down into the foliage. The vegetation tickled her nose so she flipped onto her back. She couldn't help but be captivated by the ominous beauty of the variegated black clouds high above her.

On the other side of the fence, living in Baunsee's old red-brick school building, abandoned by students and teachers decades ago, were the Gilmans. The head of the house was Edward, a reclusive and well-educated four-time divorcee. Living with him was a high school-aged son.

As the locals told the story, Edward was a college professor from a high-class northeastern family and had been fired from every teaching position he had held. The reasons: habitual drug use coupled with soliciting more from struggling coeds than extra class work. His opulent and shamefaced family had banished him from the east, and purchased Baunsee's abandoned school, refurbished a major portion of it, gave him generous access to the family wealth, and there he was to stay.

His presence though, had blown up a tempest far more damaging to the family and the village than the aftermath of his unwise choices. The oldest of Edward's children, Andrew, returned home after earning a college degree and built a meth lab in the attic of the old school. He was caught and was now in prison.

The saga had forever connected the Gilman family to illicit drugs. The reputation was the reason the intrepid fourteen-year-old Misty Wendell was lying in a pasture across the fence from the drug dealer she was sure had her beloved friend Sonny murdered.

Tired of the rock, or dirt clump, or whatever it was pressing into her back, Misty rolled over, pushed herself up, and crouched behind the fence. Right knee planted in the rich Illinois soil, torso bent forward, head erect, she pushed aside the wild clematis covering the fence so she could look through. Before her loomed a gigantic black citadel, a castle with its sole cone-roofed turret pushing high into the cloud-filled sky.

Edward's remaining child, Noah, who was intellectually disabled had been Misty's playmate when she was younger, and she had been inside the old school on numerous occasions. If she could get into the deteriorated portion of the structure where Noah and she had regularly played, Misty would have access to the entire building and could find what she was looking for.

Misty reasoned that the feeble glow of the small light over the back door could not reveal her movements. No inside lights were shining through the darkened windows, and no detectable sounds were coming from inside. Through the shadows she could see the outline of the rusty fifty-gallon barrel she and Noah had climbed on and used as a throne. It also served as the stand they used to climb in and out of a window in the abandoned section of the building.

The breeze strengthened, swirling the dead leaves, whipping the trees and along with it stoking the intense anger festering in Misty's heart. *Sonny's dead! Gilman had him killed! I'm gonna get 'em! I've got to! I've gotta do it for Sonny!*

Nature's boisterous movement of air and Misty's resolute action came simultaneously. While the wind did what it had done since the beginning of time, Misty's rage did what it had done far too often in the girl's short life: pushed circumspection out of the picture. She sprinted to the building, pressed her shoulder against the rough bricks, and froze. Except for the muted panting, the night was quiet following the stiff gust of cold wind.

Misty mounted the barrel. The rusty top started to give way under her weight, so she shifted her feet to the rim and stood upright. Pulling the unfastened bottom of the plywood window cover away from the sill, she stuck her head and shoulders beneath. Thanks to Noah, and the hammer he got from his father's toolbox, not one jagged piece of glass protruded.

Misty reached into her pocket and removed one of the two small penlights, and pointed it into the blackness. She saw the broken-down boys' bathroom she remembered. Could the larger version of herself still squeeze through the window?

The plywood held back by her head, her elbows on the sill, hands grasping the bottom sash, she stood on her tiptoes and pushed with her arms. Finally, on the third heave, she elevated herself enough to push her shoulders though the window. She inched forward and extended her right hand down the inside wall to grasp the piping.

Her position stable, she paused. *Now what,* she thought. When she was a kid, she wasn't afraid to hang onto the pipes with her hands and let the rest of her body flip over to land feet first onto the floor. Noah had shown her how, and she had performed the trick without hurting herself, most of the time anyway. Now, the mere thought of the trick scared her to death. But there was another problem: her hips were too wide to fit through the small bathroom window. She turned sideways, wriggling back and forth, edging her hips forward.

In a split second, unexpectedly, Misty Wendell, on her first ever attempt at breaking and entering, found herself within the building she had targeted. As her body slammed to the floor, backside first, she screamed curse words at the darkness. In seconds, afraid of exposing her presence, she forced her mouth shut.

Dust filled her nostrils as she found herself seated among the cobwebs inside a long-forsaken men's urinal. Her legs were awkwardly propped over a pile of boards lying before the row of latrines.

She had to get up! Her pants had caught on something as she tumbled through and were pulled almost down to her knees. Checking with one of the penlights, she also found the lower eight inches of one of her trouser legs was hanging by a narrow strip of cloth around a seam.

Using one of the useless old flush valve handles to help her stand, she pulled up her slacks, rid herself of the torn part of her pant leg, and leaned back against the urinal. She needed time to assess the damage to her bruised body.

While she did that, she also became reacquainted with the long-forgotten creaks, moans, and bangs of the old building.

Misty didn't like the delay. She had to get moving, was pressed onward by a sense of urgency. Feeling her way with her hands, she left the bathroom and climbed the creaky, old wooden staircase, fearing someone would hear with each step.

On the upstairs landing, she paused and waited. She stood motionless in the pitch black, relying on her ears to assure herself that she was still in the clear. All she needed to do was make her way to the other end of the hall. Then she would check the secret wall compartment where Noah's brother had stashed his marijuana. Noah had shown her where it was and what was in it. It would be easy to get Pastor Dave to convince the police to look for the drugs, and then tell the cops that Edward Gilman had threatened her friend Sonny. Pastor Dave was such a pushover.

Everyone, even Sonny's family, knew he smoked marijuana. He did it all the time. She had smoked pot with him at least three times. As soon as Sonny told her that Edward Gilman was after him she knew it had to do with pot. Anger welled up inside her, but she squelched it— she had a job to do. She was the only one who could put the monster behind bars.

Misty took another step and the floor squeaked. At the funeral some cousin of Sonny's who'd been in jail for burglary advised her to walk next to a wall and the floor would not squeak so much. Her next two steps didn't seem to make as much noise. She took a step, then paused, then another step, and another. She found herself beside the long window on the left, which had once provided those in the upper hall a view down into the gymnasium. She looked but saw only blackness.

She continued forward, but before her weight could be shifted to the foot in front of her, she heard a premature sound, a creaking noise. She froze. Had someone else taken a step? She listened, ears tuned to catch the slightest sound. There was nothing. She heard only the background noises of a building growing older by the minute. Uneasy, wanting this done with, she continued.

One step, and another step, and another . . .

Powerful arms suddenly clamped around her abdomen, pinning her arms to her sides, and lifting her body off the floor, holding her so tightly she could barely breathe.

Misty was being carried, toted like a passel of groceries. Whisked through the black hallway without pause, across the hall, through a dimly lit classroom now filled with weight-lifting equipment, then on to a mezzanine where there was just enough light to see the lavish interior of a home still familiar to the girl, but which seemed so out of place in tiny, backward Baunsee.

Her apprehension and journey to face the consequences of her outrageous dark-of-night intrusion had been so swift, and only now was she beginning to reason enough to scream, to kick and flail.

"Poppie! Poppie! Come see what I got!"

The voice, though deeper and more mature than when she heard it last, was familiar. It was her childhood playmate, Noah. Misty became silent and stopped struggling, as she had no more need to fight back against someone who could be controlled in a far easier way. Manipulation, a necessary and well-practiced survival technique throughout her abusive childhood, had led to a brand new plan in seconds. She had learned how to pull her former friend's strings a long time ago.

Chapter 8

The silence of the night was shattered by loud, repeated ring-tones from their house phone. At first, Dave thought he was dreaming. The persistent ringing quickly convinced him otherwise. Though the portable phone was on his side of the bed, he allowed its assault upon his ears to continue. Barb rolled over, grabbed his shoulder, pushing, pulling, shaking . . .

"Get the phone!" she shouted. Louder, "Dave, wake up and get—"

"Hello," Dave said, the receiver pressed to his ear. Out of courtesy for his wife, he braved the nighttime chill of the house. He pushed the warm covers aside, set his bare feet onto the carpet, and on the way out into the hallway glanced at the glowing red numbers on their alarm clock, which read 2:12 a.m.

"Reverend Brady?" an unfamiliar voice said. Dave detected an accent; New England popped into his groggy mind.

"Yes, this is Reverend Brady."

"This is Edward Gilman. I'm so sorry to phone you in the middle of the night. I've got a situation over here that for some reason seems to involve you." He paused. "Frankly, I don't even know how to explain what's going on. You see, this girl Misty is here and—"

"Oh no!" Dave responded. He was fully awake now. He moved into the living room to make sure Barb couldn't hear. "Did she get into your house . . . I mean, break in?" he blurted, not realizing how revealing his words were. *Good God,* Dave thought, *the crazy kid did it.*

"Is something wrong with the kids?" Barb shouted from the bedroom. She was a worrier, and he knew he had to respond or she would get up and come out.

"Just a minute," Dave said quietly. Covering the receiver with the palm of his hand, he looked down the hallway and shouted, "No, nothing like that! Church stuff!" He put his ear back to the receiver and heard silence, the cold stillness of justified suspicion. "Hello? You still there?" he asked.

"I'm here. And yes . . . yes, she did," Edward said. "How on earth could you have known anything about this?" His brogue was definitely upper class New England.

It was Dave's turn to pause. *She told me she wouldn't do this.* "Well, Misty told me she was going to do something stupid like this, but I assure you I didn't know details. I tried hard to convince her not to do whatever she . . . I mean, I talk to people all the time in confidence and . . ."

"Okay, okay!" Edward huffed. "But since you do know something about this, would you please come over and help straighten it out? You see, she knows my son Noah. She used to come over and play with him. And after we caught her tonight, and I was about to phone the police, Noah had a royal fit. When I told her I was going to call her mother, she started wailing, and my son chimed right in with another tantrum. She only wanted me to get in touch with you."

"Let me get dressed and I'll be right over. You live in the old school, right?" Everyone in the village knew the Gilman family lived in the old school, but Dave wanted to confirm.

"Correct," Edward replied. "Come to the front door."

Dave turned on the hall light on his way back to the bedroom. As he put the receiver back on the charger, he told Barb a family in town was having a problem and needed his help.

"In the middle of the night?" Barb exclaimed, perturbed. "Can't it wait till morning? Who is it?"

"The Gilmans," Dave replied. In the darkness he saw Barb's head jerk in his direction. "Really?" To avoid follow-up questions, Dave made quick work of gathering his clothing and went to the bathroom to dress.

112
***

Dave stood before a beautiful dark-stained hardwood door accented with fancy black metalwork. Not seeing a doorbell, he used the iron dragonhead doorknocker. He waited and was about to knock again when the door opened. Before him stood a muscular broad-shouldered teen wearing a Sponge Bob Square Pants pajama top, the bottom tucked in a messy fashion inside the Western belt holding up his jeans.

Dave started to introduce himself but was interrupted. "I see you!" the teenager said. Dave didn't know how to respond. They stood in the cold air staring at each other.

"Bring him in, Noah!" someone shouted.

The young man didn't move. "I see you walk . . . I see you walk with your girl too," Noah said.

"Oh," Dave replied, "you mean in the mornings. Yes, I walk right by here four times a week." He smiled. He knew about the Gilmans' intellectually disabled son. "You sure get up early, Noah."

Noah took Dave's words as a compliment and smiled. Without a word or signal to Dave as to what he should do, the boy turned and started up the short staircase. Dave entered and closed the outside door, noting how thick and heavy it was. The boy led him through a small entry hall that had a white-and-black-tiled floor, high ceiling, with deep red curtains and what looked like an original landscape oil painting, a piece of art one would find in a museum or upper-class mansion anywhere in the world but Baunsee, Illinois.

Noah slid open the tall wooden doors, then paused to slide them closed after the two had passed through.

Dave stopped short. He was in a huge high-ceilinged great room with a gorgeous circular staircase at the center. The striking hardwood masterpiece punctuated at the bottom and on each side by three giant crystal candelabra. Off to his left was a monstrous ornate old-world-style fireplace, but no fire. Extending on each side of the fireplace was a row of life-sized gilt-framed original oil portraits with ornate mirrors separating each painting.

In front of the fireplace—the only fully lit part of the room—were two leather corner couches. Between them was a huge low-carved antique oak coffee table, which was covered with a messy assortment of magazines and books. Glimpses of the darkened section of the room to the right of the staircase, below the mezzanine, revealed classy wooden bookcases filled with books.

And there was Misty, sitting on one of the couches with her head in her hands. Noah had joined her as soon as they came in.

Dave was in awe. *Why would someone with this kind of money want to live in Baunsee? Why would someone with* such a huge, beautiful home on the inside choose to live with such a trashy, unkempt exterior? Was this family hiding something? Was Edward Gilman a kingpin in illegal drug trafficking? Or was Edward, as most in town thought, just a socially soiled old man from a super-rich upper-crust East Coast family who wanted to keep him away from their high-class friends back home? As puzzling as the situation was to Dave, he still thought the local suspicions to be a better stab at the truth than Misty's assumption about some kind of criminal enterprise.

"So sorry you had to come out at this time of the night, Reverend." Edward Gilman stepped out of the shadows and jolted Dave back into the late night's surreal purpose. The host, whom Dave had heard of but never met, approached with his right hand politely extended for a handshake. He hadn't bothered to get dressed and was still wearing slippers, pajamas, and what looked like a pricey silk robe. He was gray-haired and balding.

"You're Mr. Gilman?" Dave asked with a smile as they shook hands.

"Yes," the man said in his East Coast accent. "Just call me Ed, please!"

"Actually, I'm glad you called," Dave said, too intimidated by his host's classy home to use the shortened form of his name. "I've been working with Misty and trying to help her."

Misty was still seated on the couch concealing her face. Noah was seated to her left, defiant, his right arm extended around the girl's shoulders.

"Before you came, I overheard this young lady and Noah mention 'pot' at least a couple of times," Edward said. "Was she looking for drugs?" The stern tone turned the polite words into an insistence.

Dave glanced at his young parishioner. "Were you looking for marijuana, Misty?" She had broken into this house, and the owner had a perfect right to know why she had done it.

But Misty offered neither word nor gesture in response, and continued to hide her face.

Dave's silent stare persisted for several seconds, then he said, "I'll take silence as a yes." He was relieved to have the opportunity to explain Misty's break-in with such a simple, clear-cut motivation, leaving out her audacious vigilante effort to pin Sonny's murder on Edward Gilman.

Misty, who appeared to be frozen in position, still made no attempt to counter Dave's pronouncement. Dave turned his attention back to Edward.

Edward looked him straight in the eye. "I'm sick of this shit! This is the second break in over the last six months, both looking for drugs."

Dave was taken aback. He hadn't heard of any types of goings-on in town, and usually rumors like that reached his ears. He had no idea how to respond.

Edward exhaled loudly through his nose. "Pastor, I had a thought after we talked on the phone—well, could I talk to you in private a moment?"

Dave accompanied Edward a few steps into the dim light.

"Pastor, I want to let you in on a little background, then I'm going to ask you to do something for me." Edward had Dave's full attention.

"First, Misty has been here before many times when she was young. She came to play with Noah, who you probably noticed is handicapped. And it was shortly following that we discovered my older son, Andrew, had a serious drug problem—that's a whole different story and I'm sure you've heard all about it. My concern is that Misty and Noah had the run of the house back then, and there's no telling what Noah showed her."

Where is he going with this? Dave's brow wrinkled.

"There was a lot of publicity in the newscasts and newspapers about my son's drug dealings, and ever since people have associated this house and my family with drugs. That was several years ago and people simply won't let it go. Misty's break-in was not the first and won't be the last," Edward paused. "I think Noah and I are in danger."

He stopped again, seemed hesitant to finish his thought. "I think this situation with Misty can be used to help us."

Dave cocked his head to one side. "What do you mean?"

Edward paused again. "I know this will sound crazy, but hear me out. Would you stay long enough that Noah can usher Misty around to look for marijuana or whatever drugs she was looking for?" His words formed a polite request, his posture and tone effectively added pressure.

Dave shook his head. "That is a crazy idea," he said. "I'm not sure what that would solve." As a youth director, Dave had learned to trust teens even more than their parents, but this was different, a criminal matter.

Edward tightened his lips. "I'm afraid if Misty leaves now, she won't come back and look at some more appropriate hour."

Dave was confused. "I'm sorry, Ed, but I'm not sure I'm following. Why would you want Misty to come back and look for drugs? What would that prove?"

"Noah knows where the hiding places are. Back when my son Andrew was being investigated, Noah helped the police find all the places where Andrew stashed his drugs—and, unfortunately, there were several. I'm not proud of Andrew's past—it has brought pain and ruin to my family—but this household has been clean ever since, and we've done everything we could to lay low and avoid any trouble. I want Noah to show Misty all the hiding spots so she can see for herself that they're empty." Edward's eyes were hard. "There are no drugs here now."

Dave understood what Edward was getting at. On the surface, it made sense. Here was an angry man who'd lost his son to addiction and crime. After all these years, his family's reputation was still the source of gossip and rumors. Maybe if a loud-spoken teenage girl went to see for herself that there were no drugs hiding in the shadows of this place, she could then pass on this information to others, and maybe the harassment would stop. But he still felt uneasy and apprehensive about sending Misty off with Noah.

Dave looked at Misty—who was still shielding her face with her hands—and then back at his host. "I didn't intend to stay. I just came to pick up Misty and take her home. This place is huge." He spread his arms. "How long do you think it'll take?"

"Noah knows this building like the back of his hand, every inch of it. It shouldn't take more than a half hour or so, I would think." Edward's eyes were unyielding.

The timing didn't sound realistic to Dave at all.

"Look," Edward continued, apparently seeing the lingering apprehension in Dave's eyes, "we have a limited budget for staff: a couple of part time cooks, cleaning and maintenance people, a part time bookkeeper, and someone to work with Noah a couple of times a week, but they're only here during the day. My family just can't see the need for a night watchman in a little town like this. But this place was broken into three times this year—and what do you suppose they were looking for?—drugs!" Edward's sense of urgency, and Dave's empathetic nature were pulling on him to concede—if Misty agreed.

"Hell, one time we even had a squatter living in one of the old locker rooms in the abandoned gymnasium," Edward continued. "Noah and I are vulnerable at night, not safe. If we have a local girl, a citizen of this town, who knows this building, and has looked for drugs, she could maybe convince the people of this area that we're clean, we have no drugs here, and people would leave us alone."

"Well . . ." That's all that Dave got out.

Edward turned to step back toward Noah and Misty but Dave didn't move. "But—will Misty be safe?"

Edward looked back over his shoulder at Dave, certainty in his voice. "Noah would give his life to keep that girl safe."

Dave gritted his teeth.

"Noah," Edward's voice was firm, "take this young lady anywhere she wants to go in this house and let her look for drugs, any kind of illegal drugs. Show her Andrew's—"

Noah, startled, looked up at his dad. "No drugs here, Poppie! We don't have pot!"

"Misty, are you willing to go with Noah and look for drugs?" Dave interjected, rather forcefully.

With a puzzled look on her face Misty paused before shaking her head, "yes".

Edward refused to let the opportunity pass, his voice was stern. "Noah, it's okay. Take Misty to see whatever she wants and be quick about it!"

Dave was startled at how Edward was talking to his son. *What a grouch! And what a mess this has become!*

Noah jumped to his feet, took Misty by the hand, and pulled her upright. "Ouch!" she shouted. "That hurts!"

Noah released her hand and looked upset that he had done something to hurt her. "Sorry, Misty-Misty. So sorry, Misty-Misty."

"Misty," Dave asked again, "are you sure you're okay with this?"

"Yes, Pastor Dave," she said.

Dave observed two things: Misty's tear-stained face, evidence of her well-practiced manipulative skills, and a bad bruise on the back of her left arm. Only the bruise concerned him.

"Come, Misty-Misty, come!" With more caution this time, Noah took her hand. As the two ascended the circular staircase, the deep tones of a grandfather clock from somewhere off in the dark chimed three times. *Please God, make this turn out ok,* Dave prayed.

Edward motioned for Dave to have a seat. As they sat facing each other on the L-shaped couch, Dave, successfully checking his heightened emotions, removed his flat cap, rolled it up, and stuffed the compressed banana shape into his left front jacket pocket. A wide assortment of magazines, from *Highlights for Children* to the *Atlantic*, were sprawled out on the coffee table in front of him.

Dave opened the conversation by commenting upon Noah's strange greeting at the front door. "Noah told me he sees me walk past here on my regular early morning walks."

Edward smiled. "His bedroom is in the turret on the east side of the building, the highest part of the old school, and it offers a great view of the village." Restless, up and down all night long, he said that his son either watched the village activity through the tower windows, lifted weights, or watched his favorite movies over and over again. "We probably wouldn't have purchased this old building if Noah hadn't fallen in love with the tower."

Edward was eager to talk, and Dave was an eager listener. From his host's own life story as a college professor, including his own drug problems as a young man, the conversation soon turned into a tear-filled session about Edward's oldest son, Andrew. He informed Dave that Andrew had been convicted of cooking meth in the attic of the old school and was now serving a long prison term.

The talk about drugs gave Dave an opening to fish for information about why Misty thought Edward had Sonny murdered. It had to have something to do with drugs. He could only imagine what sort of stories she had concocted in her brain. Setting his "counselor" hat aside for a moment—contrary to his professional training—he preyed on Edward's frustration about his family and drug rumors. "I think Misty thought our local murdered boy, Sonny Wigg..."

At the mere mention of Sonny's name, Edward's continence transformed. His laugh cut Dave off mid-sentence. Leaving behind his perfect grammar, but not his high-class accent, Edward spat out, "That little shit! That lazy, good for nothing little... bastard! He ripped me off!"

Dave was shocked and didn't know what to make of his host's reaction. Edward's anger, however, led to the exact information he was seeking.

Edward had hired Sonny to do a week's work with Noah to relocate old student and teacher desks, tables, and other equipment from areas in the school where Edward had decided to remodel.

"The little thief came one day—just one day—and snookered Noah into doing most of the hard lifting, which I didn't know 'til later. And he gave me a sob story about how he and his mom had no food in the house. The slick, little flimflammer talked me into giving him his whole week's wages, and then he never came back. He wouldn't answer my calls, just disappeared. I talked to the kid's mom twice, and she begged me not to press charges, so I promised I wouldn't. Involving the law would just hurt her anyway and do nothing for her impish, little brat, even if he was arrested. I don't give a damn about the money, but the lazy, little shit took me, and it galls me to let him get away with it."

Dave didn't like to be "taken" either, and he could understand Edward's dislike for the experience, but he was once again shocked at the man's over-the-top reaction. *Edward could use some anger management training,* he thought.

In terms of Sonny's work record, a few others in town who had hired Sonny to do a job—paint or mow a lawn or something—were not happy with the result. Dave was mostly upset about Tina's loss, and he couldn't help but feel sorry that Sonny would never have a chance to change and grow. But could Edward really have had someone killed for that? *Not likely,* he thought, *even with Edward's foul disposition.*

Dave successfully diverted his host to another subject in an effort to calm him. That worked well for Edward, who droned on, but not so well for Dave who put himself in danger of drifting off to sleep—perhaps he did doze off a bit. Suddenly, Misty and Noah had returned.

Words dripping with sarcasm, Edward said, "All right, Misty, empty your pockets. I want to see all the drugs you found. Put them right here!" He leaned over and slammed his hand on an empty spot amidst the magazines on the coffee table.

"No drugs, Poppie. We can't have pot here!" As Noah spoke, Misty sheepishly looked away.

"Are you sure there's nothing here, Misty?" Dave interjected, attempting to hurry their departure.

Edward pointed his finger at Misty, his voice firm, "Listen, young lady, you owe me now. I could have called the police and had you arrested but I didn't. Now you do something for me: tell your buddies at school and the people you know in town that we don't use illegal drugs, we don't have drugs here, and we don't sell drugs!"

The pronouncement was followed by an awkward silence.

Dave looked at Edward, then turned to Misty, "Okay, if our host will excuse us, I think we had better get you home."

Edward wasn't finished. His eyes, directed at Misty, cut through the tension-filled air. "Will you do what I ask, Misty?" His voice still had an edge.

She nodded her head.

"I want to hear it, young lady!"

Dave needed to get her out of Edward's house. He grabbed her arm gently.

Looking away from their host, Misty pursed her lips and offered a curt, "Yes!"

* * *

The passenger side door of Dave's car slammed shut, and a mute and unresponsive Misty sat inside with her arms crossed.

Dave got into his car and started the engine. They drove through the shallow valley to Misty's home in silence. It dawned on him that someone could see him with a teenage girl in the middle of the night, and a wave of anxiety washed through him. He stayed focused as he drove her home, hoping no one would see them.

When he pulled to the side of the road beside Misty's house, he left the engine running. Misty unlatched her door.

"Wait, Misty," Dave said. "I'm stunned. I can't believe you actually did this! What on earth were you thinking?"

"Well", Misty said, "when I used to play with Noah he showed me where his brother hid his stash of marijuana. I wanted to make sure that's still where they hid their pot. If it was in that same place I could tell the cops—maybe get you to tell the cops—where it was and they would know Gilman was a drug guy and arrest him."

"I thought this was all about Sonny's murder?"

"Ya, once I got Gilman arrested, then I—you—could tell the cops Gilman threatened to kill Sonny and they would check and get him for the murder."

That's a fourteen year old's logic, Dave thought to himself.

By the car's internal light Misty saw Dave's puzzled expression. "Gilman murdered Sonny, I know he did 'cause Sonny told me Gilman was after him, afraid the old man would have him killed. He's not going to get away with it, Pastor Dave, I'm not going to let him!"

And a Marine Sargent's determination, Dave concluded silently.

"Why would Gilman be after Sonny?" Dave asked.

"It had to be some kind of drug thing."

"Sonny told you that?"

"Well—no, but what else could it be?"

Dave sighed, shut off the engine. "Listen to what I'm about to say, Misty. Mr. Gilman told me he was angry with Sonny, but it had nothing to do with drugs; it had to do with work Sonny had agreed to do that he never completed. Sonny had gotten paid and never finished the job he was hired to do. Gilman was angry, but to a wealthy man like him it was nothing to have someone killed over."

Misty listened in silence, looked off into the surrounding darkness.

"Let me get this straight, Misty, you wanted to get Gilman arrested for possession of illegal drugs, then collude with me to get him charged with Sonny's murder?"

The two sat in silence, Misty caught, Dave too dumbfounded to ask the next logical question.

"Misty, did you find the hiding place you were looking for?"

"Yes."

"Were there drugs there? You said you didn't find drugs."

"It was empty," Misty looked down into her lap as she answered.

Dave had no idea whether Edward was, or was not involved in illegal drugs. He was anxious, however, that Misty leave the Gilman's alone. "Who knew you were going to do this tonight, Misty?"

"No one."

"You foolish girl . . . if Mr. Gilman was responsible for Sonny's murder, he could have made you disappear and no one would have ever known what had become of you." There was a pause. "But here you are, alive and well! You found no drugs in the house! Don't those things tell you something?"

Misty was silent for a moment, then said, "I don't think he killed Sonny now." And added in a more firm voice. "I really don't."

"You're through bothering the Gilmans, right?"

"Yes." She looked over at Dave as she surrendered.

Fear over his present situation once more hit Dave full in the face. He needed to get Misty out of his car before someone saw them. "You need to go in." His voice was polite but firm.

The girl didn't move.

"Misty, you've got to . . ."

Misty leaned over the divider between the two front seats, slipped one of her arms under his, and hugged it to her. As she did so, Misty laid her head on his shoulder. "You saved me tonight, Pastor Dave! Thank you!"

At that precise moment, a car came around the corner and slipped past, illuminating the interior of Dave's car for a second or two.

Dave panicked. He jerked his arm free, climbed out of the car, and started around to the passenger side. He needed to get her out! Before he could get to her door, she had pushed it open and jumped out, leaving the door wide open. With angry, uneven steps, she hobbled across the street toward her front door. She was furious.

Dave slammed the passenger door, hard. Not even looking to make sure she got into her house before he left, he sped off, tires spitting rocks as he disappeared up the street. At the moment, he didn't give a damn how angry the rebellious little brat was.

Chapter 9

An uncomfortable silence enveloped the kitchen as Dave finished giving his hostess an account of her daughter's audacious overnight adventure at the Gilmans. Though justified in sharing this information—Misty's safety was the most important concern—he couldn't help feeling like a rat.

In addition, despite his efforts to present himself as professional and in control, he sensed that spilling the story to Phyllis Wendell had come across as an apology for keeping Misty's confidence in the first place. He did not want to convey such a message.

Eyes filled with incredulity, ill-humored Phyllis, wearing a faded kimono-style housecoat, fumed at being so completely left out of a situation in which her daughter had engaged in such risky behavior. Dave could see the anger in every crease of her face. He normally took Phyllis's ill humor and periodic shunning in stride, but this Tuesday morning he wanted to avoid a rift. He wanted something from her.

As the awkward silence continued, Dave's eyes, in an attempt to avert the uncomfortable glare of the irate matriarch sitting across the kitchen table from him, tracked the smoke rising from the ashtray. Her cigarette had burned to the filter.

This is not the first time Dave had been in this position. The other matter was a little congregational dispute that had nothing to do with Misty. He was not afraid of Phyllis. Once she settled down, he found her to be quite reasonable. It was just uncomfortable for him to get from here to there.

Phyllis followed Dave's gaze and snuffed the cigarette out. She then took her time removing another from the pack, lit it, took a drag, and blew the smoke from the right side of her mouth, unconcerned about the path it took across the table.

"Now she already broke in the Gilmans' place and I can't do nothin' 'bout it," Phyllis's gravelly voice offered. "Whaddaya want from me?"

Dave avoided Phyllis's eyes as he calculated just how to continue. "Well, I'm here to make a request on her behalf. I'm going to go see Michael at the county jail this afternoon, and Misty has asked to go. She can't go unless you accompany us or give her written permission to see Michael with me." Dave was disappointed that Misty had disregarded their agreement for her to lay low. But the sheriff had good reason to allow the visit.

Phyllis's response was delivered with both the force and darn near the volume of a shotgun blast: "I ain't goin' to no jail to see that damn kid!" Her forehead creased. "Michael Early? The guy who killed her friend?"

"Is accused of killing her friend," Dave corrected. "She heard me say I was going to visit Michael at the jail and asked me if she could go with me."

"Why?"

"It's what Christians do, visit people in jail." That was an obvious answer, but he went on. "The sheriff told me that Michael was depressed and thought it would be good for his morale if I came to see Michael and Misty came with me." Dave stopped there. He hadn't told anyone, not even his wife, that Michael had made a crude but close-to-successful effort to take his own life. The sheriff was concerned.

Uncharacteristically, Phyllis said nothing, drinking it all in.

Dave heard the TV in the living room click on. The familiar voice and cadence of Scooby Doo, with excessive volume, shattered the silence.

"Jasmine!" Phyllis screamed at her eight-year-old daughter. "Turn the ga'damn TV down!" She looked into Dave's eyes when she swore, daring him to challenge her choice of words.

Then Phyllis jumped to her feet, hurried into the living room, and shut the TV off. Jasmine screamed. Through the doorway, Dave watched the child reach right around her mother and click the TV back on.

"Then you keep it down so we can talk," Phyllis said in a stern voice as she lowered the volume.

Phyllis sat down in the kitchen and took another drag from her cigarette. "So lemme get this straight. Ya blindside me with what Misty did last night, and now you want me to let you take her to see the guy who may have killed her friend." She cocked her head to the side, lifted her shoulders, her solid steel eyes hurling an unflinching gaze at Dave. "Makes perfect sense to me."

Dave ignored her sarcasm. "To be honest, Phyllis, I never thought the sheriff would allow me to bring an unrelated minor for a visit. I was certain of it." He looked down at the tabletop. "But I didn't know Michael was depressed."

As cartoon characters shouted and tension-laced music flooded the kitchen, there was another pause in the conversation. *This is awkward,* Dave thought. He couldn't blame Phyllis for being upset about the situation. Misty was her responsibility. But as everyone in town knew, Phyllis was just one of those people who was difficult to deal with.

Inexplicably, Dave sensed that his host's attitude was shifting in a more amiable direction. He began to feel more positive vibes, even a hint of a smile on Phyllis's lips.

"Thanks for helpin' us get the car fixed before it got cold," Phyllis said. She took a drag on her cigarette and made a better effort to blow the smoke away from Dave. "The church wouldn'a helped us again if it wasn't for you." She looked off at the mess in the sink and something within her changed again. "What Misty did last night was dangerous, whad'n it?" There was fear in her voice.

Dave nodded. "Yes. I knew she was up to something, but I swear I didn't know who or where."

"Are you sure you want Misty to go with you?"

"Yes." There was no hesitancy in Dave's voice. "I promised her I would ask the sheriff if she could come along with me, and he not only gave his consent but made a special appointment for when there would be no other visitors. I think I can help lift Michael's spirits, and the sheriff seems to think it would help a lot if Misty came along. There you have it."

"When she wakes up, I'll ask if she wants to go," Phyllis complied.

After Dave detailed the arrangements for this afternoon's visit at the jail for Phyllis, she took him by surprise again. "Thank you," she said. Dave welcomed both the expression of appreciation and the sincere tone Phyllis used to deliver it. But he was not sure what she was thanking him for. He questioned her with his eyes.

"I mean, for gettin' Misty outta the mess. Gilman may not be a drug dealer, but he's a grouchy old fart. When she used to play with Noah, she came home in tears several times. I couldn't see why she kept goin' back."

Dave stretched his hands across the table toward his hostess. "Let me pray with you, then I've got to go."

Phyllis put down her cigarette and extended her hands. Dave grasped them and prayed: for safety for Misty, and for guidance and strength for the alarmed and shaken mother.

Dave stood. Jasmine, the TV blaring behind her, was leaning against the kitchen wall next to the living room doorway. The faded image on the front of her oversized T-shirt was un-discernable among the folds. Her hair was a total disaster and the stretched-out neck of the T-shirt exposed her shoulder.

"Pastor Dave!" she squealed.

Jasmine flew to him and threw her arms around his middle. As he leaned in to her hug, her arms stretched upward to surround his neck. She gave him a quick kiss on the cheek. Then, as quickly as she had appeared, she retreated back into the living room.

* * *

A few hours later, Dave was parked in the dirt parking space in front of Misty's house. It was 1:20 and the drive to the county jail took about twenty minutes.

Misty was usually prompt, but not today. After repeated glances at the front porch, he considered going to the door. Then she appeared. She cautiously stepped off the porch onto the broken-up sidewalk, and then, favoring her right leg, hobbled toward the car. He went around to the passenger side and opened the door for her. Ignoring the strong whiff of some kind of cheap perfume, he asked, "What in the world happened to you last night?"

"'Fell through a window and I don't wanna talk about it!" Both strident tone and volume reinforced the prohibition.

"Have you called your doctor?" Dave asked.

"Mom doesn't think I broke noth'n but said I need ta see a doctor if it don't get better."

Dave got back behind the wheel but did not turn the engine on. There was another issue that needed to be addressed. He chided himself for not thinking to give Phyllis the dress code for visitors to the county jail.

Misty caught his glance at her clothing and baited him. "There's nothing wrong with how I look! Nothing!"

Dave sighed. "There is a dress code for visitors to the jail," his voice was firm, his words flowed evenly, "and for women it cannot be a mini-skirt and a blouse with a plunging neckline."

Misty swatted her comeback. "You've gotta be friggin' josh'n me!"

Dave shook his head. "Misty," he said in soft voice, "you cannot wear those clothes to visit prisoners in the county jail. Your legs must be completely covered, and you can't have an open front like that. Those aren't my rules, but those of the sheriff's office. Please go back inside and change."

Misty huffed and grunted as she heaved her body out of the car and slammed the door behind her. She stomped toward the house, anger visible in her every move.

A few minutes later, Misty emerged in a long sleeve knit cotton sweat outfit Dave had seen Phyllis wear numerous times. Dave was relieved. He was afraid she would have reappeared in something covering just a little more of her but would still be questionable.

Misty slid into the front seat, huffing and puffing. "Here's the note from Mom," she said, practically throwing it at him.

Engine humming, the two slipped north on Route 99 toward Gillespie in a landscape made blue-gray by one of the intermittent clouds scattered above. The brightness of direct sunshine drew Dave's eyes ahead to a line of colorful trees and a vivid white farmhouse.

As they rumbled over the railroad crossing just north of town, the panorama of which they were a part was transformed. Their car was now speeding along in sunshine, a line of fields on either side, all divested of their produce, all displaying vivid yellow or a less-striking brown stubble giving evidence of their previous bounty.

As they ascended the north side of a tree-filled vale, Dave broke the silence. "I'm a little afraid of what you're going to say to Michael, especially if you become convinced he killed Sonny." This situation was an unknown. He usually went to visit people in jail by himself.

"I won't say nothin' to hurt him," she promised. Her tone was a little on the cranky side. He had come to know her pretty well and was confident at least a part of her desire to go along was just plain nosiness.

Another surprise. "I'd be depressed if I was him," Misty said. There was a pause. "You think he really did it?" The waspish overtone in her voice had disappeared.

Dave was guarded in his answer. Teenagers were impressionable, and he didn't want to say anything that would sway Misty, so he kept it as vague as possible. "We're just going to see Michael to help lift his spirits. We're not there to judge him. We can only trust the law to do what it was designed to do."

"I know," she said quietly.

"When we get in there, just let me take the lead, okay?"

"Okay. I've never done anything like this before."

Dave was taken aback by Misty's immediate compliance. Misty, along with the many other troubled kids he had tried to help during his ministries, were incapable of trusting adults—not parents, not preachers. He paused to soak it in.

"About last night," he pressed his luck, "I thought you had agreed you wouldn't—"

"I said I'm sorry! I'm sorry!" The repeat of an apology she had never originally made was louder. The strident tone had returned. "You got me back though," she jabbed. "You told Mom!"

Remembering his own twisted childhood, and his oft-rejected attempts to help dysfunctional young people over the years, had elevated him above personal disappointment. He didn't harbor negative feelings about her promising not to take matters into her own hands and then invading the Gilman home.

"What I was trying to do in talking to your mother had nothing to do with 'getting you back.' I told your mother because it's my job as an adult and spiritual advisor to protect you and make sure that you're safe." Dave spoke softly. "I feel you're being honest with me now . . . thank you, Misty," he said.

Their discussion about how she was going to conduct herself at the jail had put his mind at ease. The truth is, Misty had let him breach the protective wall she created around herself to a greater degree than any of the other teenagers he had tried to help.

Content for the moment, Dave silently watched the Midwest scenery fly by and focused on the artistry of ever-changing color, sunshine and shadow, on a partly cloudy autumn day.

* * *

The visit with Michael was not face-to-face, as Dave had experienced on occasions when he had made such a call by himself, nor were they siting in a booth behind thick glass that separated prisoner from visitors. He and Misty found themselves in an audio/visual room connected to Michael through high-definition TV, microphone, and speaker.

The orange-clad hulk on the screen reflected a dismal sight: little remained of the bruises Dave saw at the arraignment, but Michael looked dog-tired, his red hair unkempt, and in need of a shave. Dave introduced himself, then acknowledged Misty.

Following a cursory glance at Dave, Michael, in a surprisingly clear baritone voice, turned his attention to Misty. "I . . . I . . . thought you were Sonny's girl?"

"Ahh . . . I really liked him, but he didn't like me like that. He liked some other girl, I think her name was Ashley?" She paused, looked down at her hands and then back up into the screen. Her voice was weak, "I don't think you . . . done anything to 'im."

As Dave listened, he was reminded of the gentle tones he had heard her use with the younger children in Sunday School. He gave Misty a few minutes to work her magic then eased his way into the conversation. "Misty and I came to see you to let you know there are people in Baunsee who care about you and your mom. Your mom asked me to stop by and see you."

The mention of Michael's mother brought a downcast facial expression and an effort to fight back tears, both speaking to the pain and fear the boy felt. *I've got to get him talking,* Dave thought.

Sensing Misty was about to say something, he reached over and patted her hand, nodding his head in Michael's direction. She got the hint to keep quiet.

Michael's eyes glistened. He paused, but then he opened up. He regretted not treating his mother as he should have, and expressed his fears about what this whole episode would do to her. Dave and Misty sat in complete silence, rapt with heart-felt empathy, almost forgetting they were communicating through a high-resolution television screen.

After talking about his mom for several minutes, Michael went silent. His burden had been lifted for the moment. Misty pushed her previous sensitivity to the side and popped the one key question they both wanted to ask, "What happened between you and Sonny?"

I'm not sure he's ready for this yet, Dave thought.

Michael was ready, however, and dived right in. "This is the truth, the same thing I told the cops. Sonny told me his mom was outta town, and he just got a stash of pot. He wanted me to bring what I had and come on over to play Bloodgift and have a joint or two."

"Bloodgift Saga is a computer game," Misty whispered to Dave.

"Yeah, so I got to Sonny's house," Michael rolled on, "and we played for a while. Sonny's a lousy-ass player though, and a sucker for the Glass Cannon Pull . . ."

Dave was lost, "That's a move in the game?"

"Yeah, yeah, kinda, it's when . . ." Michael went on for several minutes, but Dave had no idea what he was talking about.

Michael continued, "Anyway, we used up all my weed—just enough for a joint—then played some more, then I wanted another joint. I asked Sonny to get his and he said, 'Let's wait a while.' We played, then I asked him again and the lying little shit said he didn't have any!"

Michael's tone of voice and body language showed escalating agitation. Dave was keeping tabs on Misty out of the corner of his eye and observed that she also was getting upset.

"I wacked the little pecker in the arm and we got in this fight," Michael's excited voice increased a decibel, "which didn't last long cause the little pussy's only half my size."

"Michael!" Misty screamed. "Ya don't talk that way when you're talkin' to a preacher!"

The girl's rebuke wrenched Michael back into the present. His startled expression turned into a smile and resulted in an apology. "Oh, I'm sorry, Pastor, I know better! Anyway, I grabbed my game controller and left. When I left, Sonny was sittin' there on the floor with his back against the wall bawlin' like—" he fished for a less offensive term to use "a tiny little baby!"

Michael was determined to finish telling them what had happened. In a calmer, respectful voice, without profanity, he continued his story. He didn't know how Sonny had gotten outside his house, and he claimed over and over that Sonny had been alive and well when he left. Michael swore he had no idea how Sonny had been fatally injured.

After Dave did some personal counseling work with Michael, he returned the floor to Misty and the two of them talked about teachers, former teachers, and students. This confirmed Dave's suspicion that busybody curiosity was a key motive in Misty's incentive to visit Michael.

As Dave started to bring the visit to a close, he suggested he say a prayer on behalf of Michael and his mom. As Michael clasped his hands together against his forehead, Dave noticed a deep blue image on his right upper arm. It looked like a tattoo of a snake, the top covered by the short sleeve of his orange jumpsuit.

Following the prayer, Dave asked Michael about the image inked on his arm. Michael, pride obvious, pulled up his sleeve to give them a better look. It showed the serpent's mouth wide open, oversized fangs dripping with venom. The snake, its sharp tail protruding from beneath the coils, looked threatening. The image caught Dave's attention; held it fast, sent his mind back to the freezing morning and the bone-chilling shrieks stopping him in his tracks.

"Is that snake an adder?" Dave asked. The young man's response was a blank look and a puzzled shrug.

There was more to Dave's question than an enduring interest in wildlife and a lifetime of watching nature videos. It had to do with Sonny's frozen scream, the last one Dave heard. As Dave knew, it was the victim's last utterance on this earth. Perhaps, Dave couldn't help but think, the police had arrested the right person.

"Perhaps . . . the police had arrested the right person."

Chapter 10

Dave's involvement in the unsettling events of the past few days had put him in a heightened state which hampered his sleep and was now propelling his sturdy legs as they carried him through the morning chill. He crossed his driveway, then, conscious of his footing, stepped onto the broken, uneven sidewalk beneath the naked branches of the neighbor's catalpa tree.

Out even earlier than usual for his Thursday morning walk, Dave looked up and down Route 99 and waited in a circle of light created by a mercury vapor lamp for a car to pass.

Crossing over the highway he saw a few small white speckles of sleet sailing helter-skelter around him. His mood was bleak, and to match, the world was literally dark, made even more so by an inky black cloud cover.

The last couple of days in particular had held both great interest for Dave, and at the same time resulted in more than his usual share of distress. His rescue of Misty had landed him in the kitchen of the unsuspecting and volatile Phyllis Wendell. His dual purpose was to frighten her with unsettling facts about what her daughter had done, and then to assuage and persuade.

And how should he characterize the trip he and his troubled young friend made to the county jail to see Michael Early? Was it a positive experience centered in Christian love? Or was it the downer of sharing time with a depressed young man awaiting the verdict of his upcoming trial for murder? It had, of course, been both.

Lost in his thoughts, Dave hiked past the peach-colored home of a young single church member, an attractive first-year elementary teacher. A Cocker Spaniel barked at Dave from its pen behind her garage.

In the midst of an even longer list of unusual events, all of them connected to Baunsee's first major crime since the discovery of Andrew Gilman's meth lab, Dave focused for a moment on just one hopeful thing. Misty was safe, in the protection of her own home, and would soon be up and preparing to catch the bus for an age-appropriate day at Wabaunsee Valley School.

But what about Michael Early? During the initial part of their visit with Michael, the young man's openness, sincere manner, and, on the surface at least, believable account of what had happened on the night of the murder had led Dave to think the boy was innocent. But the sight of that tattoo on Michael's arm had driven Dave toward the opposite opinion.

On the drive to Misty's home after their visit at the jail yesterday, Dave had driven by the scene of the crime. Both sets of eyes observed the yellow police tape that still encircled the place where Dave had found the dying boy. He could never forget those blood-curdling shrieks. That last strange-sounding outcry might well turn out to be the ultimate confirmation of Dave's suspicion about Michael.

Had the "adder" become a nickname for Michael after the tattoo had been inked onto his shoulder? Was Sonny's scream an attempt to tell the world who had struck him down? To date, Dave had found nothing, heard nothing, to corroborate what he thought, yet it was the only way he could make sense of both the unusual scream and the tattoo.

Just before Dave had dropped Misty off at her home yesterday, he had asked if she had ever heard anyone call Michael "adder." She looked puzzled, just as Michael had when he was asked the question, and shook her head. It had been quite common to hear the kids call him "Big Red" because of his hair, and at least once Misty said she had heard Sonny call him "Flare" because of his hot temper. Misty had never heard him referred to as "adder."

Back into the freshness of the present morning, Dave's legs propelled him past a row of older homes. He had conducted the funeral services for both a husband, and a year later the wife, who had occupied one of those houses.

Making a turn onto the last street in town, the street where Sonny had lived, Dave remembered another tidbit Misty had told him. One time when Sonny and Misty were high, Sonny had given her a clue about where his stash of marijuana was hidden. According to her, Sonny bragged, "Only me and the birds know where I keep my stash."

Unsurprisingly, Misty admitted she had tried to find Sonny's hiding place, but to no avail. She figured, and still believed, Sonny had hidden his marijuana somewhere in or around the emu enclosure across the street from his home. She had secretly searched the area twice but found nothing.

Dave stopped on the road in front of the enclosure for the oversized birds. The larger female stood just inside the fence, and the smaller male stood behind her and to the right. He heard the distinctive low boom-boom noises from the animals as he approached. The jumbo-sized birds stared at him as he attempted to look beyond them into the unpainted gray wood shelter. It was not light enough yet to see much of anything.

Dave turned and looked across the street, around Tina's house, at the large mature sycamore tree in her front yard. A few orange-yellow leaves remained on the branches, and a thick layer of them gave the yard an attractive varicolored surface. The large tree abounded with niches suitable for nests, but none within easy access from the ground.

As he surveyed the small red-brick home, a movement caught his eye. A sparrow, small and fast, had disappeared under the roof. He moved a little closer. Toward the back of the house he saw a couple of small, darker places in the white-painted soffit. They looked like broken boards. A hiding place there would make much more sense to him than the emu enclosure across the street.

But what difference did it make? Everyone knew Sonny used the drug. According to Michael, the police knew that marijuana had brought the two boys together, which then caused the fight that ended in Sonny's death. Another in a growing list of confirmations that Sonny possessed and used the illegal substance told them nothing. Sonny was dead. Michael was in jail. And the only connection that Dave could make for Sonny's last strange scream was Michael's tattoo.

One of the emotional uplifts Dave enjoyed while on his morning walks was a regular encounter with two untethered Golden Labs. The older one—he guessed the mother—moved slowly and was content to patiently await her turn for scratches and pats as the pup jumped and frolicked around their friendly visitor. The mom stood silent and satisfied as she enjoyed the acts of affection her pup refused to slow down enough to receive.

Just four blocks from his home, by this time in a better frame of mind, Dave looked at the extensive old village school—especially Noah's watchtower—with brand new eyes.

* * *

Dave peeked through the glass panel in the door of Shelly's Restaurant and saw Barb with one of the couples they were to meet for lunch. They were seated in their usual spot at the large round table in the center of the small restaurant.

When Dave entered, he received the customary threefold welcome every customer was met with at Shelly's: the ting-a-ling of the cheerful bell over the door, a welcoming smile from Shelly, who was peeking through the serving window to see who had come in, and, best of all, the fragrance of Shelly's wonderful home-cooked food.

The couple with Barb stood as Dave approached, Jeff for a grin and handshake, and Gloria for a warm smile and hug. "Norman and Denise are on their way," Gloria offered. Dave left a seat between Barb and himself so the three women could assume their customary places together.

Dave plucked the laminated menu from behind the ketchup and mustard bottles in the black metal condiment rack. "So, now that Norman's crops are safely gathered in, he'll be fit to be around?" he asked Jeff. It was a good-natured jab at a beloved friend who had a tendency to become a bit testy around planting or harvest time. They all chuckled.

Shelly, who was standing at a nearby table, shouted something about an order to her father, the cook, in the kitchen. "I have a question about Joel," Gloria interjected. They were studying the minor prophets in the Thursday Bible study, and Gloria and Barb had been at the church for this morning's session.

"Shoot," Dave invited.

Just then, Denise and Norman walked through the door, bringing a burst of cool air with them. The temporary bluster of fall air led to a second round of warm greetings.

Seated together, the men talked farm, and the women, soon bored with discussion of the area's primary endeavor, talked in softer tones about church matters. Dave was more interested in the agricultural discussion and heard the dry weather had lowered corn production in Illinois. This year's crop looked like a good one, but it would be less than last year's record.

As they were in the process of telling the waitress what they wanted, a burst of uproarious laughter from a nearby table drowned out the moderate, congenial banter of the room. The exultant uproar came from five or six farmers and one woman, four of the men wearing Bib overalls.

Dave was curious about what caused such laughter, but he focused on getting to the point when he could take a brief leave of absence from his table to greet the other diners. Today, he was interested in one diner in particular.

When everyone had finished ordering, he left his table to greet the other patrons. Never shy, and teased about being a politician at heart, Dave would take the time to speak to everyone whether he knew them or not.

The moment Dave came in, he noticed Tina and another woman around her age seated at a small table against the north wall. He felt the desire, the need, to try to connect with her. He knew she was hurting on the inside and couldn't resist an attempt to help, despite Tina's repeated rejection of his previous efforts.

As Dave walked toward Tina's table, the woman she was with reached out and took his hand. She introduced herself as Tammy, a childhood friend of Tina. She told him how much she had appreciated Dave's words about Sonny at the funeral. Dave's mind had been full of other things at the service, so he remembered little more than seeing her there, but thanked her for the compliment.

As Tammy told Dave a little about herself, she kept glancing at Tina and Dave assumed she wanted Tina to enter the conversation. Tina sat in silence, her eyes fixed on her soda.

The conversation with Tammy was brief. After an awkward silence, she used her straw to play with the ice at the bottom of her glass, allowing Dave and Tina time to chat.

Dave looked at Tina and said, "Hi, Tina, I'm glad Tammy's come to see you. Helps to have a friend to talk to, doesn't it?"

"Ya," she sighed, "I needed to talk to someone." She looked up at Dave when she spoke, then looked back down at her drink. "Maybe . . . maybe next time I need to talk, I could see . . . you. But I . . . just don't know what to say."

Dave was both surprised and pleased at the suggestion. "You don't have to say a thing right now, Tina—nothing. But I would be glad to talk when you want. I would like to get to know you a little better."

There was another pause. After some mental gymnastics—should he, shouldn't he—Dave went with his gut and proceeded to the next step. Doing his best to combine spontaneity and earnest concern in a relaxed tone, he asked, "Would you like a hug?"

With no hesitation, Tina was on her feet and the two embraced, holding each other tight for several seconds while sounds of small-town banter, the scent of home-cooked food, and the clatter of kitchen utensils filled the room. It felt good to Dave, and this time Tina didn't become frightened and feel the need to thrust him away.

Chapter 11

Misty shoved her school PE clothing—odor and all—into her small locker. She plopped down on the bench. A cluster of girls were giggling and changing out of their gym clothes. Locker doors were being slammed. Voices echoed. Misty always lagged behind, waiting for them to all go away.

She perched her right ankle on her knee and straightened a white sock. As she did, she couldn't help but see the somewhat distended flesh from her thigh pressing against the three slits in the leg of her jeans. She hated her fat and despised gym class because her weight was on open display.

Gym was fun today, she had to admit, and the thought brought a smile to her lips. They'd played Capture the Flag Basketball and it was wild! There were four teams playing at the same time. They used four balls and all four of the gymnasium baskets and earned flags rather than points. She never caught on to all the rules, but she got into the game anyway and loved the chaos. It had been a good distraction.

The three days following Misty's school suspension had been surreal. She assumed it was because everyone knew about her friend Sonny's murder. Mrs. Francis had offered her an especially warm smile when she came in Wednesday morning, which was weird. The associate principal had taken her into the office and offered her condolences, then set her up with a social worker. Mrs. Francis's demeanor—her whole way of dealing with Misty—was uncharacteristically kind and respectful.

There had been a pleasantness in all of the teachers' voices. As for her classmates, the few girls who didn't normally ignore her were silent rather than offering catty remarks or flipping her the bird. The boys couldn't care less and were into their own stuff, as usual. Misty had been disconcerted by it all. She didn't know what to think, but there was a heavy feeling in the air, and she kept expecting the other shoe to drop.

She pulled on one of her boots that was slightly too small and laced it up. The black leather boots were worn and scuffed, but she loved them. She had used her babysitting money to snatch the pair up for a fraction of the original cost at one of her favorite thrift shops.

Three girls finished dressing and joined the others in the gym. Misty, thinking she was now alone, was startled by a cough. There was scuffling on the other side of the olive-drab-colored lockers. It was probably another fat girl, she reasoned. All the fat girls lingered after class, just like Misty.

Misty hated school. She fantasized about ditching "the Hole," as she referred to it, never to return! The kind treatment she had received over the last three days had made no difference. She knew it was all going to go back to the way it was. As a matter of fact, she was going to put things at Wabaunsee School back in proper order. A fiendish grin came over her face. She was going to get Kiara alone and beat the crap out of the little bitch.

Absorbed in her own thoughts, she heard another noise, but needed to hurry. *Shit,* she thought. *I'm gonna be late.* The unusual silence in the now-empty locker room shouted in Misty's ear at the same moment her nimble fingers tightened the bow in the frayed black laces of her second boot. She looked up, and adrenaline rushed through her body. She jumped to her feet. Kiara was standing all by herself at the end of the bench.

Anger infused her entire being. At first, Misty was stunned, then euphoric, then filled with caution after remembering the ambush outside of the girls' bathroom. Jaw clenched, she took a quick look behind her, then another to make sure. It seemed that they were alone. It didn't make sense. With just the two of them, she could whip the trashy imp with one hand tied behind her back.

"Well, well, well, if it ain't the candy-ass pussy from Gillespie. Hi, bitch," Misty scowled, keeping the volume down. She didn't want anyone to hear and to come to Kiara's rescue.

"I'm not here for a fight, Misty, please! I just wanna talk." Kiara's body was tense, her jaw tight, open hands raised, yet ready for the action she was asking to avoid.

Posturing for attack, Misty took a quick step forward, but to her surprise, Kiara stepped back. What was going on? Kiara never backed away, no matter what the odds.

A puzzled look on her face, Misty cautiously stopped. Once again she suspected her archenemy's friends were lurking somewhere in the locker room ready to join in an attack from hidden positions. But she could see nothing, hear no suspicious sounds, detected no danger to herself.

"Listen, Misty, I don't wanna fight ya no more." Kiara's face was blank. She spread her arms in surrender and took yet another step back.

"Ya sure?" Misty snapped. "You and your friends take me by surprise, bust my ear, get me suspended. Now you're alone, just little ol' you, and all of a sudden you don't wanna fight no more?" Misty, eyes flashing fire, cocked her head to one side and taunted the pint-sized blonde before her. "Ya think I'm stupid?"

"I mean it, Misty! Please . . . stop! Let's don't do this no more!"

The sincere expression on Kiara's face, the words, the fervent tone, and her body language were baffling to Misty. Her face twisted into a scowl. From the minute Kiara had walked into this school and sidled right up to Ryan Shaw, Misty had hated her—still despised the little tramp. And up to now, Kiara hated Misty, got her into trouble over and over. Did Kiara really think she was going to get away with all that she had put Misty through?

The girls silently stared at each other. Misty's angry eyes bore straight into her combatant's face. Kiara's eyes showed no trace of surrender but also held a desire for a future different from the past.

Then a sadness came over Kiara's face. "Your frien' got shot."

"What?" Misty paused. "What of it?" Something totally out of the ordinary was happening and Misty did not have a clue how to respond.

"My frien' got shot too," Kiara said. Her face was tortured, and she took another step back.

Misty could feel the agony in her ordinarily tough opponent's voice. She could see the hurt in Kiara's eyes, and it cut into her heart.

In Misty's life—repeated former attempts by sincere counselors, teachers, and pastors, honest endeavors to try and help her deal with childhood abuse and neglect, the taunting, teasing and belittling by peers and adults—nothing had gotten through to her. But those five words from Kiara's mouth went straight to Misty's heart and melted away both her anger and intention to take revenge upon a world full of pain.

The deafening sound of the bell flooded the building. Frozen in place, not reacting at all to the closing bell, the girls jumped at the sound of Mrs. Francis's voice. Initially standing in the locker room doorway, concealed from the girls by a row of lockers, the associate principal, face expressionless, stepped into view. "You two don't need to go anywhere. I like the track you're on, so please carry on. There are no other PE classes coming in, but I'm staying right here. If you aren't comfortable here, we can go talk in my office."

Misty was jolted back to the old familiar reality. She had been set up by Kiara and Mrs. Francis!

"Shit!" Misty said under her breath, then, "You're gonna pay for this you little—"

"I didn't know she was here, I didn't!" Kiara said in a desperate plea. "I asked to use the restroom, and when I got out of class I came in here all by myself. I swear no one else knew."

"Misty," Mrs. Francis intervened, "I didn't know about this ahead of time. One of the students saw you and Kiara in here alone, told Ms. Stokes, who immediately sent for me. I want you two to work your differences out together, without my intervention."

Doubt was broadcast in Misty's frown and her eyes were moist with the hurt of yet another disappointment. She could only view them with suspicion. Life had given Misty little reason to trust anyone.

Kiara's eyes were filled with tears. "We lived in South Chicaga when my frien' got shot," she managed to get out. "I was seven, and my frien' Tiana was seven. We played with our dolls on the back porch. Her doll was black and only had one arm." She paused to pull herself together and looked away. "I still got it, and look at it, and hug it for Tiana."

Misty was in shock. She could see the pain in Kiara's eyes. The dagger of loss stabbing into Kiara's heart now pierced her heart as well.

"One day when Mama was workin', we was on the back porch playin', and there was shooting in the alley behind our house. Gramma yelled for me to get in the house fast and hide under the bed. I yelled at Tiana to come, and then I was scared and I ran. I thought she was behind me, but when I got under the bed she didn't come. The gunshots stopped, and then I heard Gramma screamin'. I ran outside and Gramma grabbed me, but it was too late. I saw Tiana layin' and there was blood . . . Tiana died!" She paused. "Right after Tiana got killed, Mamma and Emmitt broke up, and we came to Gillespie to live with my other gramma. That's why I'm here."

Silence followed, the sober-faced girls struggling with internal turmoil. Misty couldn't believe Kiara's story. In just a few short moments, she was connected to Kiara in a tragic way forever. She wanted to say something but was afraid to show what was going on inside.

"I'm sorry about your friend Tiana," she finally said, breaking the silence.

"I'm sorry 'bout your frien' too, Misty. I'm sorry for what I done ta you. I'm so sick of this shit. I'm sick of killin'. Sick of fightin'. Sick of hurtin'. Sick of hurtin' even when I win. I wanna stop this, Misty! Please, let's just stop!"

Misty looked at the floor. She knew Kiara was right; they needed to end this once and for all. Anything was better than silence, so she came clean.

"I took your homework. It was sticking out of Mr. Cobbler's textbook. I nabbed it and took it to the bathroom, and when I saw what it was, I tore it up in little, bitty pieces and flushed it down the toilet," Misty said. Tears burned her eyes. "I'm sorry! I'm sorry! I'm sorry!" she shouted. She paused. Her voice took on a tone of genuine sincerity. "Kiara . . . I really am sorry."

More silence.

This was all too intense, and Misty couldn't stand it. Someone had to bring an end to it. So she stood up straight, folded her arms across her chest, and stared at Kiara. "I'll never be your sis, Fart Breath!" she said with a stiff grin.

Kiara looked startled, then spontaneously responded to Misty's smile with a grin.

"Misty," Kiara said, broadening her smile, "I don't wanna be your friend neither." She paused and the smile gave way to a more serious look. "I'm sorry for what I done ta you too, Misty. I just don' wanna fight no more, please. We have to stop!"

Misty hesitated, then nodded in consent.

Chapter 12

It was a clear, cold morning in mid-January and Dave was returning to Baunsee from Peoria. He had just exited the freeway and was now on a secondary road that led to Illinois Route 99 and home.

Two inches of snow the day before left the fields on either side of the road fresh, clean, and white. In the midmorning sunshine, the black clumps of Midwest soil, cleared of snow by the winds, stood in crisp contrast to the pure white surfaces surrounding them.

Always on the lookout for beauty, recompense for the boredom of driving a route he had traversed time after time, Dave came to the top of a rise and his eyes were met with miles of snow-covered paddocks reflecting a beautiful silver-blue surface. It looked like an alluring inland sea, the uneven ground the swells, the rows of exposed soil clumps the waves.

The holidays behind him, the dutiful pastor was back at his work. The visit to St. Steven's Hospital in Peoria was to pray with the Evans family before Pete's knee replacement surgery, and then to the ICU unit to see a gravely ill grandmother who was not a member of his congregation, but whose granddaughter had attended for three years. The granddaughter, an energetic and active young woman, along with the other relatives present in the hospital room, had been glad to see him, thankful for his concern and prayer.

His next step for this Friday was to eat lunch with Barb and Emily, their visiting fourth-grade granddaughter, and then a shorter afternoon trip in the opposite direction to Gillespie to see a church member who was a hospital patient there.

After lunch, and subsequent to Emily demonstrating her budding literary skills by reading Grandpa a children's book, Barb gave him the Gillespie Times open to an article about the Sonny Wigg murder trial.

The coming court proceedings were no surprise to Dave as he had just had a second pretrial interview with Angela Fenton, the state's attorney. She had been just as impressive in person as she was at Michael's arraignment. In this second interview, she wanted to know every detail of everything he knew and had a way of pulling it all out into the open.

The net effect of the article was to make Dave feel guilty. He had visited Michael at the jail one more time, a couple of weeks after his and Misty's visit, but had not been back since, and had not seen or heard anything from Sandy. The deepest remorse was due to Dave's failure to following up with Tina after his commitment to do so in their brief visit at the restaurant weeks ago.

* * *

Dave made a brief stop at the church, still intending to continue on to Gillespie. There for only a few minutes, he stood in his hat and jacket as he looked over the bulletin for next Sunday's worship service. In the weekday silence of the church building, typically a welcome sanctuary for Dave, his guilt about neglecting Tina elevated to the point he could no longer ignore it.

Tina had an unlisted number, so if Dave wanted to talk to her, his only choice was to knock on her door. Parked on the street in front of the deteriorating red brick home, Dave hesitated to get out, instinctively he looked for the yellow police tape suspended above the fresh snow even though Larry had told him a month ago he had removed all trace of it.

Tina's car was in the drive, eliminating his wish to simply leave a note on her door. He knocked. Nothing. He knocked a second time a little louder and was preparing to leave a note when the door opened. Tina stood there, her eyes puffy and her cheeks stained with tears. She beckoned for him to come in, stepped back, buried her face in her hands, and wept. He put his hand on her shoulder, she stepped toward him, and in silence he put his arms around her and just let her grieve.

She motioned for Dave to follow her into the living room. He removed his hat and jacket on the way, placing them on the opposite end of the sofa where Tina seated herself. Retrieving a chair from the kitchen table, he positioned himself facing her.

She talked, he listened. Out of the corner of his eye Dave caught sight of the house phone he had used to get help for Sonny. It brought a rush of memories about that traumatic early morning discovery and Dave had to forcefully keep himself from glancing in that direction. A trained and practiced counselor he soon saw only Tina, heard solely what she was saying to him, periodically nodded to let her know he understood or asked a question to help her clarify what she meant.

Ready for the catharsis, she poured out her soul for well over an hour, exposed her life to him, did not hold back, in the final few moments struggling to relate her bitterness about the murder of her only remaining child. Her anger was not directed toward the accused murderer but the vicious God who had orchestrated it all!

When Dave sensed Tina had unburdened her soul as much as she was capable of, she became defensive and acted as though she expected Dave—or God—to do something bad to her because of her openness. It was a horrible unfounded guilt.

Dave's response was to assure Tina this was all confidential, that no one else would hear a word of it from him. When it became apparent to her that he was ready to leave and only wanted to have a brief prayer with her, she thanked him for not lecturing. She then shared how much the judgmental attitudes of Christians had hurt her over the years, how much she distrusted church people, and how every other time she had shared anything with a preacher it had ended in a lecture which left her feeling even more hopeless and angry. It was obvious Tina didn't like the church, or church people, in particular preachers. She went on to confess that Dave was an anomaly of some kind and she couldn't figure him out.

After listening, Dave violated his own rule against talking about himself when counseling. He told her that he had grown up in a home dominated by a violent alcoholic father. He told her about his guilt for not getting out of bed and defending his mom, and, paradoxically, the anger he felt toward his mother for not getting his father out of the house. He told her about his own anger against a harsh, unfeeling God who, despite Dave's fervent prayers, did not stop his father from drinking.

Tina was stunned. And when Dave was through talking, he was frozen in the mire of the confusing feelings talk of his childhood always stirred up. Neither of them could think of anything further to say.

As Dave put on his jacket, he severely chastised himself. He had come to lighten a grieving mother's burden but in the end had dumped his own sordid childhood on the poor woman. He had to find a diversion, had to fix it. There had to be a way to put her and her issues back into central focus as he left her.

"Do you know where Sonny kept his marijuana?" he blurted clumsily. Tina's head jerked in his direction, face blank, and didn't answer. *God, what did I say?* Dave thought. Then felt compelled to go on, "Misty said he hid it in a spot only he and the birds knew about." *Lord in heaven! That made it worse.*

Tina's eyes flashed, her face turned crimson, and the muscles in her jaw tightened. "Birds? Birds? What birds? I knew he had some here, and I don't want it here . . . anywhere near here! I want it away from here . . . now!"

In response, Dave, cowed by this lapse in judgment, uncertain of how to respond to his agitated hostess, could think of nothing to do other than rattle out the rest of the story. "I know the emu pen across the street has been searched twice and there's nothing there, but on my walk I go by here and I saw a place, an opening in the soffit on the east side of your house where something could be hidden."

Still shaken, nerves frayed, Tina said, "I searched and searched, over and over again. Mom and Dad searched, the police searched, none of us could find it!" There was a pause, and then, "But we all searched inside the house." She repeated, "I don't want pot anywhere on my property! I want someone to get it away from here . . . now! Please, get it out of here, Pastor!"

"Maybe I should go find Greg . . ."

"No! No!" Tina screamed, her shrieks so loud everyone on the block could hear. The terrified woman buried her face in her hands and cried. The impact of what he had disclosed hit Dave full force. Those naïve words offered as information landed upon Tina's ears as something else. A threat? Temptation? A reminder of who she was? A revelation of who her son was? Whatever it was, his words were somehow fraught with peril for her inner being.

"Okay, okay, I'll go look," Dave replied. "Is it okay if I look?"

Tina nodded. "Yes . . . yes. I need you to find it and get it outta here, now," she sobbed.

"Tina . . . I don't want your neighbors to see me nosing around outside your house by myself. Will you please go out with me?" Dave also wanted a witness in case he did find something.

Tina searched Dave's face as she pulled herself together enough to respond. "I can go with you, Pastor, but it scares me to death. What if we find it and someone sees us?"

"I can vouch for you, Tina, but I won't go out there and look by myself." The more he thought about it, Dave had become even more leery of finding it. *What will I do with it if I do find it?* He kept his thoughts to himself.

Without saying a word, Tina retrieved a red jacket from the coat hooks along the wall behind her. Dave noticed Sonny's heavy orange-and-black winter coat hanging on a hook beside it. With shaking hands, Tina put on the jacket. "I guess this is the only way I can be rid of it," she said.

"If there's anything there," Dave added. It was still possible that there wasn't any stash at all.

"Are you sure you don't want to ask the police or sheriff to come?"

"No! No way!"

Tina moved to the door and went out. Dave followed behind her.

As they rounded the corner of the house, his eye caught sight of the section of the yard where he had found Sonny. Dave was instantly wrested from the present moment and froze. He saw darkness, falling snow, a snow-covered body, and heard screams. His mind obsessed upon that last strange outcry. The visit with Michael at the jail convinced him it was an accusation. Was it? Could Michael Early, in a fit of anger, really have done this thing?

Tina, ahead of him, stopped under a hole in the soffit above her head. "I avoid this side of the lawn," she said softly, after the brief pause.

Two sparrows, one right after the other, burst noisily from the opening above her head and flew off. Tina screamed, bringing them both back to their purpose in the yard.

As they looked up at the black hole, Tina remarked, "Not very wide, is it?"

"Maybe the boards are lose, but how on earth would Sonny have gotten up to it?" Since the ground sloped downward toward the back of the house, it was the corner of their home highest above the lawn. The edge of the roof looked like it was at least ten feet from the ground.

"Well, Dad's ladder is . . ." Tina looked along the bottom of the red brick wall. "Where is it?" she asked, startled. "It's an old ladder Dad made a long time ago, and he doesn't even use any more. It's always right here." She pointed.

"I'll look around the house," Dave offered.

"I could go in and call Dad," Tina said.

Dave pulled out his phone and handed it to Tina. As she phoned, Dave circled the house. No ladder anywhere.

"Daddy didn't take the ladder," Tina said when Dave rejoined her, "and he has no idea where it went." She handed Dave's phone back. "The neighbors wouldn't have taken it without asking first. Maybe a storm blew it somewhere?"

Dave continued to survey the property, but there was no ladder.

"I want to see if there's anything up there," Tina continued, her mouth set in a hard line, "and I don't want anyone else to know about it." She marched down the incline toward the tree-filled ravine behind their home.

Dave hurried after her. He felt responsible for her upset. The temperatures had elevated throughout the day, so the snow had been melting, exposing the grasses along the slope. There was still snow under the trees and bushes. Two sets of eyes searched on down into the tree and brush-filled valley.

"There it is!" Tina pointed to a section of leafless brush halfway down the hill.

"You wait here," Dave said as he moved down the slope, almost falling backward on a slippery patch of grass. The ladder was lodged against a sturdy dogwood bush. Grasping one end, he had some difficulty dragging it back up into the yard. Almost to the top, out of breath, he dropped the ladder and paused to catch his breath. "We never would have been able to see it through summer leaves and bush," he said.

"Maybe the wind blew it down there?" Tina suggested as a moderate gust of wind blew through the branches of the taller trees rooted in the vale below.

Making no comment on the speculation about the wind, Dave sized-up the ladder. "Looks like about a fourteen footer. Larry did a nice job on it."

He and Tina worked together to bring the ladder the rest of the way to the house. After noting the location of the wires, Dave propped it up against the edge of the roof. In silence, as Tina watched, he moved it a little at a time, first one way, then the other, until it was situated where he thought he could reach up under the soffit.

"Let's see if there is anything in there." Dave carefully stepped up the ladder.

"Watch out for the birds," Tina warned.

Dave had to come down, move the ladder a little more to the left, and then climb back up. Reaching between the side rails and rungs, he explored the soffit around the holes and found two loose boards. He pushed them up and peered in. It was dark, and he could see only bird droppings, weed straw, and feathers. Maneuvering so he could see from a different angle, he spotted something white further back. Able to put his hand on it, his fingertips got a grip and he pulled it out into the light.

It was an opaque square-shaped Tupperware container with the tan lid fastened in place and covered in bird droppings. There was something inside. He tossed it to the ground and climbed down. They stood over it and stared.

"I don't think we should open it," Dave said. "As a matter of fact, I don't even think we should clean it up."

"I don' care." Tina's voice quivered. "Just get it outta here now. Please!" There was desperation in her voice.

Dave looked into Tina's tear-filled eyes. They were his mother's eyes, begging her son for help. He had failed to rescue his mom as a child. He would not let her down again.

"Do you have a brown paper sack?" Dave asked. Tina disappeared into the house and returned with a paper grocery sack. Dave understood Tina's strong reaction, both her fear of the law, and the absolute havoc such substances had wrought in her family. Half of her life had been flushed down the toilet, a daughter killed in a drunk driving accident, a son torn from her because of a fight over marijuana. *Or,* Dave thought, *was she just terrified by her own weakness?*

Dave opened the sack, turned it upside down over the container, and lifted the plastic container using the sides of the sack, flipped the sack right side up, allowing the container to drop into the bag.

"You sure you want me to take this?" he asked.

"Yes! Get it out of here!" He could hear the angst in Tina's quavering yet resolute voice. He suddenly feared for himself. *What if I get caught with it?*

Going straight to his car, he put the grocery sack into the trunk, slammed the lid back down, waved to Tina, and got in. A gust of wind shook the naked branches of the large sycamore tree in Tina's front lawn as she entered her front door.

What in the name of God am I doing? he thought and drove away.

Chapter 13

Dave adjusted his tie and buttoned his sports jacket as he approached the towering hardwood courtroom doors. Without conscious thought, he unbuttoned the jacket as he moved through the center aisle of the all but empty visitors' gallery. The state's attorney, Angela Fenton, professionally dressed, held the gate in the bar open for him. She was attractive, in her mid-thirties, and her bobbed blonde hair, ends tucked just below her chin, encircled a welcoming smile and its pleasant partner, a whiff of Chanel No 5.

After the court clerk administered the oath to Dave, he seated himself in the witness chair. Judge Cramer had short white hair and was wearing a black robe, the top unzipped to expose a brown-striped tie against a yellow dress shirt. The only people in the visitors' gallery were Sandy and her parents. *Not one reporter here,* Dave thought. *No one cares about kids like Michael.*

As Dave glanced at the court recorder, the judge prompted him to offer his name and occupation. All eyes focused on him. His mouth was dry. *Ridiculous!* he thought.

After years of public speaking, he should be capable of delivering his testimony without such distracting anxiety.

"Should I call you 'Reverend' or 'Pastor'?" the state's attorney began. She stood behind the lectern between the tables for the prosecution and defense, her fingers curled around the outside edges of the podium. Her voice was pleasant, but she now offered a more professional expression. Her eyes alone offered a smile.

"I would prefer 'Pastor'," Dave pushed through his dry lips.

The judge intervened. He looked in the direction of the bailiff and asked him to bring water for the witness.

During the brief ensuing pause, Dave scanned the refurbished antique cherry-wood courtroom. The newspaper article from months ago about the conclusion of the county's renovation project had failed to capture the true beauty of the stately old courtroom.

His eyes were drawn to the trio of men seated at the defense table. Michael Franklin Early, the defendant, looked well-groomed and was wearing a gray long-sleeved polo shirt. Michael had come to regard Dave as a friend, and his eyes searched Dave's face for some hopeful sign.

After Dave had a sip of water, the state's attorney began her questioning.

"Pastor, would you tell the court what you were doing on the morning of Tuesday, October twenty-fifth, of last year?"

"I was taking a walk . . ." Dave had to pause to clear his throat, then took another sip of water. "I was by myself because it was cold, and my wife doesn't walk with me in the late fall and winter, especially when it's snowing."

"There was a snowstorm that morning," the state's attorney interjected, "correct?"

"Yes, there was. In Baunsee we got about four inches." He lifted his hand to measure out the depth with his fingers.

"Anyway, I try to walk four mornings a week. I was walking my usual route around Baunsee when I heard this horrible shriek." He paused. "In our little town, we're used to coyotes, and they can make crazy sounds easily mistaken for those of a human, but this wasn't like any coyote I ever heard. A moment or two later I heard another scream, so I left the street to go see where it was coming from. That's when I found Sonny lying in his yard."

"You are referring to Sonny James Wigg, the victim in this case?"

"That is correct, he was lying in his yard covered with snow."

"Sonny Wigg, the victim, was alive when you found him?"

"Yes . . . alive enough to yell out anyway. Right after I got to him, he screamed again."

"He cried out a third time?" the state's attorney clarified.

"Yes, but the last time it was different, like he was trying to say something—a word—but I couldn't make sense of it."

The state's attorney leaned forward and rested her elbows on the lectern. Her serious expression and intense gaze communicated keen interest. "This is important, Pastor Dave. I will want to know more about that special third cry in a few minutes, but let's continue for now. What happened after you found the victim?"

"Well, I ran to the house looking for Tina, Sonny's mother. She wasn't there, and her car wasn't there, so I went on in, found their phone, and called 911."

"You went inside the Wigg home to call emergency?"

"Yes," Dave said. "I didn't bring my cell phone with me on the walk, which really ticks my wife off." The side remark brought a slight smile to the face of the state's attorney and aroused a quiet chuckle in the jury box. Sandy and her parents, three sets of frightened eyes, had no interest in humor.

"You went into the house once?" State's Attorney Fenton said.

"No. After I got back outside I thought Sonny should be covered up, so I went back in and took blankets from one of the beds."

"You were in the house twice, then?"

"Correct."

"Which rooms were you in, Pastor?"

"The phone was on the wall in the living room, and I went into a bedroom to get the blankets."

"You were in two rooms, then?"

"Yes."

"Did you see anything unusual inside?"

"Yes, I did," Dave continued. "It looked like there'd been a fight."

"Objection, Your Honor, conjecture!" At the defense table, there were two people with Michael. William "Bill" Early, a cousin to Michael who was studying law, and who was being supervised by one of his university law professors, Dr. Robert Schultz. Bill had made the objection.

The judge looked down at Dave. "Confine your testimony to what you saw, Pastor. Don't speculate."

"Well, I saw furniture pushed out of place, the coffee table was upended with two broken legs, and there was trash everywhere."

"What can you tell us about the condition of Sonny when you found him?" the state's attorney asked. "He was covered with snow for one thing. But when I tried to brush the snow off, I saw blood on my hand. He was bleeding from the back of his head."

"Was there a lot of blood?"

"I thought so, couldn't tell for sure," Dave answered. "I start my walk before dawn and it was just getting light."

"Go on," the state's attorney urged as she leaned an elbow on the podium. "What happened next?"

"It seemed everyone came at once," Dave said. "First the local ambulance, and right behind them, the sheriff, highway patrol, and then, after a time, our local policeman, Greg Anderson, came. He'd been out of town."

"By just looking at the victim, did you have any idea about what could have caused such a severe wound to his head?"

Another objection arose from the defense table. "Calls for speculation!" The motion was sustained.

"Withdrawn," the state's attorney submitted as she took a quick peek at a paper on the lectern before her. "Did you see anything on the ground around the victim—a club, a rock, or any other instrument that could have caused such a wound?"

"No . . . nothing." He paused for a moment. "When I tried to get up to go to the house, though, I stumbled over a rock under the snow and hit my knee."

The state's attorney's eyes registered curiosity. She paused, then asked, "Tell us more about the stone in the yard."

"Well, I didn't pay much attention to what I tripped on at first, but it was just a two-or three-inch stone."

"But it was protruding above the ground high enough that you caught your foot on it."

"Correct. But another thing . . . it seemed to be attached to the ground, part of a larger stone buried in the lawn."

"Okay." The state's attorney's eyes narrowed. "Did you see any other wounds, bruises, or injuries on the victim?"

"Yes. There were a couple of cuts on Sonny's face—one looked a bit deep, but didn't appear to be bleeding much."

"After seeing the disheveled furniture inside the house, did you have any thoughts about where the victim's facial wounds could have come from?"

"Objection!" Bill called out. "The counsel is calling for speculation again."

"Logical inference!" the state's attorney countered, as her fingers tightened around the edge of the podium. She looked at the judge.

After a thoughtful pause, the judge allowed the question.

"What were your thoughts then, Pastor?"

"Sonny, and someone who'd been with him, had been in a fight," Dave said in a bland voice. He had concerns about both families, hurt where they hurt, but growing up in a violent alcoholic family had conditioned him to swallow his feelings.

The state's attorney placed her elbows on the podium and made a tent of her fingers just below her chin. "When you first found Sonny, was there anyone else present, or did you see any sign that someone else might be present?"

"No." Dave shrugged. "Some neighbors came out to see what the commotion was all about after the emergency people got there."

"Did you see or hear anything in the house that would lead you to believe there might be someone else in the home either time you were inside?"

Dave was a bit startled. The thought hadn't crossed his mind. "No. I just saw the messed-up furniture, and I smelled what I thought was marijuana . . . but I saw no one else in the house."

State's Attorney Fenton stood up straight. "I found no mention of the scent of marijuana in the house when I read the statement you gave to the police."

"I . . . I certainly wasn't trying to hide anything," Dave stammered. "There was just so much to absorb . . . I was so upset. I guess I didn't even think about it when I talked to the officers. It did come to my mind when it was all over, but I knew the police would be going into the house—they know a lot more about such things than I do."

"Do you know what marijuana smells like, Pastor?" she asked.

"Yes," Dave responded. "When I first went into the ministry, I worked with the youth at an inner city church, and at one point I attended a police-sponsored workshop with others who dealt with city kids. When the session was over, the officer in charge burned a small amount of marijuana in a tin can and allowed those of us who didn't know how it smelled to take a quick sniff."

"So," the state's attorney teased, offering the witness a sly grin, "you do know what marijuana smells like?"

"Yes," Dave said with a triumphant pitch to his voice. "And that's what it smelled like in Sonny's house."

"Pastor, I understand at a later date that you found marijuana at the home of the victim, an illegal substance you subsequently turned in to the sheriff's office. Would you tell us how you found it?"

Dave paused, then turned to look at the judge. "Your Honor, I had gone to the Wigg home to console Sonny's mother, Tina Timkin—she uses her maiden name, Your Honor—and while I have no objection about sharing the circumstances of finding the marijuana, I would like to keep in confidence anything about the conversation I had with Ms. Timkin."

The judge looked at the state's attorney, then at the defense lawyers, and asked them the same question: "Do you have any objection to keeping the pastor's conversation with the victim's mother confidential?"

Neither side objected. The judge directed the state's attorney to continue.

State's Attorney Fenton lifted a brown paper sack from the table. "Your Honor, before I continue with the questioning, I would like this exhibit marked into evidence." She walked to the defense table and handed the bag to the opposing attorneys. They removed the Tupperware container, opened it, took a sniff, and after replacing the lid, returned it to the sack.

"Your Honor," State's Attorney Fenton continued, "may I approach?"

With the approval of the judge, she took the exhibit to Dave and asked if it was familiar to him.

"Yes. This is the container of marijuana I found at Sonny's house and the grocery sack Sonny's mother gave me to put it in."

"Are you sure?" The state's attorney's eyes searched Dave's face.

Dave leaned forward to take a closer peek inside the sack. "Yes, I'm sure. This is what I found and turned over to the sheriff."

"Your Honor," the state's attorney continued, "I ask that this illegal marijuana, found by the witness at the home of the victim on January seventeenth of this year, be entered as evidence."

The procedure complete, the state's attorney turned back to the witness. "Please fill us in, Pastor. What led you to this discovery?" There was a subtle change in the tone of her voice and the slant of her brow reminding Dave of the toughness she had displayed at the arraignment.

"One of the young people in Baunsee told me Sonny had given them a clue about where the victim hid his stash," Dave said. "Since I pass the victim's house on my regular morning walks, I couldn't help but look for a place fitting the description. I saw a place, and later, when I went to make a pastoral visit with Ms. Timkin, she gave me permission to look. I searched and found the container of marijuana you showed me, which Ms. Timkin then asked me to remove from the premises."

"Pastor, let's back up even further. What made you suspect Sonny used marijuana in the first place?"

"Well, the victim's family members—and I would prefer not to reveal names—told me that the victim used marijuana."

"Okay, and the person who gave you the clue to Sonny's hiding place was not a family member?"

"Correct."

"And as I understand it, you took the marijuana to the sheriff's office in Gillespie?"

"Yes. I took the Tupperware container to the sheriff's office on the same day, immediately, as fast as . . . well, as fast as I could legally drive!"

A second audible chuckle spread throughout the courtroom.

"Pastor Brady," the state's attorney continued, "you have now testified to the odor of marijuana in the victim's home the morning following the alleged crime, testimony from family members that the victim used the substance, and then to finding a container of marijuana at the home of the victim. Is all of that correct?"

"Yes, all of it is true."

"You also testified that you saw no one in the Wigg home, or on or around the premises, when you found the victim in the snow on the morning of October twenty-fifth, and while you waited for the first responders to arrive? Is this accurate also, Pastor?"

"Correct."

The state's attorney paused to check through the papers, and took her time selecting the one she wanted. With a furrow in her forehead and a more stern look in her eyes, she looked at Dave. "Moving on, Pastor Brady, tell us about your relationships with the Early family, the accused and his mother."

"Well, before all this happened," Dave began, "I didn't know any of the Early family, although I had seen Michael walking around town a few times late at night."

At the mention of his name, Michael, who had been slouched over with his elbows on the table, leaned back, crossed his arms, and looked at Dave. His right foot, ankle crossed atop the left, began to jiggle in apprehension.

"After Michael's arrest," Dave continued, "one of my church members who works in the Baunsee gas station introduced me to Sandy while I was having coffee." As Dave spoke, he saw Michael turn his head to take a quick glance at his mother.

"Sandy Early? Michael Early's mother?" the state's attorney quizzed.

Dave glanced past the counsel and out into the visitors' gallery. Sandy looked tense. Dave's eyebrows drew together; he felt for poor Sandy, but that concern was mixed with curiosity about where the state's attorney might be taking him.

"Yes," he answered. "Sandy had come into the Quick Shop, and she—I mean, the clerk in the gas station—thought Michael's mother might want to talk to someone, so she introduced me to Ms. Early. And again, I would prefer not to talk about my conversation with Ms. Early except for one thing. I offered to make a pastoral visit with Michael at the jail. She seemed eager to have me make such a visit and urged me to go."

"Let me make sure I'm understanding this," the state's attorney said. "The defendant's mother, Ms. Early, wanted you, in a pastoral capacity, to go see her son who was being held in the county jail?"

"Correct," Dave responded.

"Pastor, did you go see the defendant?"

"Objection, Your Honor!" Dr. Schultz made the motion as he rose to his feet. "As the witness has already implied, conversations between an ordained pastor and those they counsel are considered to be privileged, 'confidential communications.' We object to any testimony from the meeting or meetings between Pastor Brady and the defendant."

The state's attorney delivered her response with equivalent confidence. "There are exceptions, Your Honor, and this situation calls for confidentiality to be set aside. Most recently, I refer Your Honor to the ruling in Anderson verses Daily in 1996. In this case, when the clergyman talked with the defendant, a third person was present; therefore, the confidentiality privilege was waived. The court compelled the clergyman to divulge information disclosed during the visit."

The judge took over. "Again, Pastor, you did go to the jail and visit the defendant?"

"Yes. I did . . . twice," Dave answered.

"Was there anyone with you when you went to the jail and spoke to the defendant?"

"On the first visit, yes. Misty Wendell, an acquaintance of Michael, accompanied me." Dave chastised himself for stating Misty's name. At the same time, he saw the deep lines of concern on Michael's face and felt a deep sadness for him.

"This young lady went into the visitation room at the Wabaunsee County Jail with you, and was present when you and the defendant talked?" the judge asked.

"Yes," Dave answered, "but just on the first visit with Michael. I went alone to visit Michael a second time . . . only the two of us then." He was starting to sweat.

The judge continued, "At any time during the first visit did the young lady leave the room so she could not hear the discussion between yourself and the defendant?"

"No. She was there the whole time. She heard everything we said."

The judge checked his wristwatch. "It's eleven-forty, closing in on time for our lunch break. Let's adjourn while I make a decision on this matter. I want to see the attorneys for both sides in my office after adjournment. The rest of you are free to get something to eat. I will announce my decision when we re-adjourn for the afternoon session."The judge looked down at Dave. "Pastor Brady, you may leave the building to get lunch, if you please. I will trust you not to speak to anyone about this court case, and not to read or listen to or watch any news concerning this trial. Do you understand what I'm requiring?"

"Yes, Your Honor."

"Good." The judge redirected his eyes to the jury box. "Court is adjourned! Be back in the courtroom ready to resume by one-thirty p.m."

* * *

After an everything hot dog at the nearby Frankfurter House on Plum Street, and a brisk walk through the downtown streets of Gillespie, Dave felt refreshed and alert. There was a caveat, however. Life in the home he grew up in had made him hypersensitive to subtle changes in those surrounding him. He had walked out of the courthouse with a growing suspicion that State Attorney Fenton had something up her sleeve. His observation of her work at the arraignment led him to believe it would be something with a punch to it. When he finished lunch and entered back into the courthouse, a wave of nausea washed over him.

A paper in one hand, eyes directed toward the witness, Judge Cramer reminded Dave he was still under oath, and then addressed the court concerning the confidentiality ruling. After reiterating the facts of the two visits with Michael to the jury, the judge made the ruling. "Since a young lady accompanied you on that first visit with Michael, nothing said during that visit can be withheld. You are not, however, obligated to answer any questions concerning the second visit. Do you understand, Pastor?"

Dave assured the judge his instructions were clear. Simultaneously, the uncertainty he felt about Michael's guilt or innocence were wreaking havoc with his emotions. Would his testimony help free a guilty man or convict aninnocent one? All he could do was to hope for the truth to come out.

State's Attorney Fenton moved to the side of the podium. She placed the papers she held on the lectern and rested her left elbow upon them. "You have testified, Pastor, that on the morning you found the victim, Sonny James Wigg, you also found evidence of a physical disturbance inside the home of Mr. Wigg. On that first visit with the defendant, did he tell you anything about an altercation?"

"Michael told me Sonny claimed to have a stash of marijuana. Sonny had wanted Michael to come over to his house and play a video game." Dave had no choice but to follow the judge's ruling, but continued to worry about what Michael was thinking. Michael's facial features betrayed nothing but deep apprehension.

"Pastor, excuse the interruption, but I want to make sure the jury understands. "Sonny, the victim, asked Michael, the defendant, to come to his house to play a video game and smoke pot?"

"Yes, that is correct," Dave affirmed.

"Okay, Pastor, please go on. What else did the defendant tell you about the encounter?"

"Michael told me Sonny asked him to bring his own marijuana."

"Hold on, Pastor, Michael brought marijuana also? Both of the young men were in possession of pot?" The state's attorney held up two fingers.

"Yes, but Michael told me he only had a little marijuana, barely enough for a joint."

"Okay," the state's attorney continued, "then what happened?"

"They used Michael's marijuana first, then later in the night, when Michael wanted more, Sonny told Michael he had lied and didn't have marijuana at all. That's what started the fight."

Dave watched the crestfallen Michael rest his elbows on the table and drop his forehead into his hands. His family, in the gallery, remained frozen in place.

The state's attorney simplified. "Both of the young men agreed to furnish marijuana, Michael kept his side of the agreement, Sonny did not. Hence, there was a fight. Is that accurate?"

"Correct," Dave responded. "What Michael said is that he fought with Sonny and beat him up and then went home. But he also told us over and over again he did not kill Sonny, and the victim was alive—very much alive—and still in the house when Michael left."

The state's attorney was quick to take the opening. "The defendant is a large man." Her words were spoken with confidence. "Jail records have him at two hundred and twenty-four pounds. Sonny, on the other hand, was small. Medical records have him at one hundred and fifty-eight pounds. Are you sure the defendant said nothing to you about Sonny running outside of the house to get away from a much larger attacker?"

"Objection, Your Honor, the counsel is leading the witness!" A disapproving scowl twisted Dr. Schultz's face.

"Sustained." The judge eyed the state's attorney. "Be careful here!"

Her point made, State's Attorney Fenton paused. "Pastor, can you be more specific about what the defendant told you about the conclusion of the altercation?"

Dave was still in the dark about where State's Attorney Fenton was taking him.

"After the fight—what Michael himself admitted to be a one-sided scuffle—Michael, just took his game controller and left. According to Michael, Sonny was sitting on the living room floor with his back against the wall as alive as he could be." He saw a glint of hope in Michael's eyes.

"Again, did the defendant indicate anyone else had joined him and Sonny at the Wigg home on the night in question?" The state's attorney's eyes were cutting into Dave like lasers.

"No," Dave repeated, "he didn't admit to anyone else ever being there."

"No one else was there to hurt Sonny—or to kill Sonny."

"Objection!"

"Sustained!" the judge shouted.

"Did the defendant give an indication of the time he left the Wigg home?"

"No, nothing was said about the time."

"Did any communication between you and the defendant, on the first visit, hint at what time the defendant left the victim's home?"

"Michael told us—Misty and myself—that he and Sonny played their game, smoked what little marijuana Michael brought, and then resumed playing their game. I don't know how much time passed, but eventually Michael wanted another joint. Sonny put him off, according to Michael, several times, but eventually confessed he had lied and had no marijuana at all. In terms of timing, that's all I can tell you because it's all I know."

"So perhaps, Pastor Brady, the fight between the defendant and accused took place close to the time you found the victim?"

There was an objection but the judge overruled it, as the state's attorney's line of questioning had to do with establishing the timing of the crime.

"I guess . . . possibly . . . I have no way of knowing for certain." Dave was being pulled down some kind of rabbit hole, could sense it, but was not in control.

"Okay, then," the state's attorney forged ahead, "we need to return to your earlier testimony about finding the victim. Tell us again, in more detail, about that mysterious third cry you heard."

It suddenly dawned on Dave where the state's attorney wanted to take him. He didn't like it, but was powerless to stop it. She had paid close attention to what he had said at their pretrial meetings.

"For you to understand what I'm going to say here, I need to tell you something else about the first visit . . . at the county jail I mean."

State's Attorney Fenton looked into Dave's face. "Please go ahead, Pastor."

"While with the defendant at the jail, I happened to notice Michael had a snake tattooed on his right upper arm. I mentioned it to him, and he pulled his sleeve up to give me a better look. He was proud of it."

The state's attorney turned to look at the judge. "I have an enlarged photo of the tattoo I would like to enter into evidence, Your Honor."

Moving to the defense table, she removed the photo from a manila envelope and laid it before the defense team.

Given permission to approach the witness stand she held the large color photo so Dave could see it. "Is this the tattoo you saw on the defendant's arm?"

"Yes," Dave's voice was confident.

"Be sure you take a good look, Pastor Brady, are you certain?"

"Yes, absolutely."

After the formality of entering the photo into evidence Dave found himself standing alongside an aluminum tripod to which the state's attorney had attached the photo.

"Okay, then, Pastor Brady. Would you tell the jury what features of this tattoo caught your attention when you first saw it, and why you connected it to the final scream the victim made the morning you found him?"

Dave shifted his weight from side to side. Sweat dotted his brow. All eyes were on him. "This may sound crazy," he began. "The tattoo is obviously of some sort of poisonous snake. As you can see, it has fangs dripping with venom and a sharp tail. It's not a rattle like a rattlesnake." He shifted his gaze from the photo to the jury. "When I saw the tattoo, it popped into my head that it might be an adder a type of poisonous snake without a rattle on its tail."

The courtroom was dead silent. Everyone, including the judge, was curious about where Dave would end up.

"You see," Dave continued, "'adder' is the only word I could think of that sounded anything like the last frozen scream I heard Sonny make. His last scream was drawn out and sounded something like: 'aaaddeeerrr.'" Face red, he felt silly as he tried to repeat the cry.

A swift glance out into the gallery revealed confusion on the faces of Sandy and her parents. Michael had an equally bewildering expression on his face. Dave still had the feeling he was being taken somewhere without his consent. Where on earth was this going to end up?

"So the names have similar sounds," the state's attorney pushed, throwing her hands in the air. "The similarity doesn't mean they're connected in a way linked to this case. There has to be another piece to the puzzle. What have you not told us?"

Dave's face was red, and his heart was pounding. "As soon as I saw the tattoo, I thought of the scream." He paused. *This is going to sound so dumb,* he thought. "I jumped to the conclusion that 'adder' was a nickname or code name for a person selling illegal drugs, or who had something to do with criminal activity. In that frozen scream, I thought Sonny, the victim, was trying to tell me who had attacked him."

The rattled pastor found it hard to breathe. He paused to take a deep breath and refused to look into the state's attorney's eyes.

"It may sound crazy," he continued, "but it's what I heard, and, for the moment at least, what I honestly thought." That would be Dave's final word on behalf of the prosecution.

The confused and meekly delivered testimony had broadcast the good pastor's self-doubts about the cursory interpretation of what he had seen and heard. The confident follow up of the state's attorney, by contrast, had all the earmarks of rock, solid truth. She took Dave's unease, his sincerity, the trustworthiness people attributed to those in his profession and bundled them together with his rudimentary interpretation of what had happened, then tossed the alleged certainty into the lap of the jury.

State's Attorney Fenton's eyes thrust her confidence into Dave's face and out into the room. "You have testified, Pastor Brady, that the defendant told you both he and the victim, Sonny Wigg, were smoking marijuana on the night of the murder, and they had, in fact, gotten together for that purpose. During the evening, however, they had a falling out involving marijuana which ended in a violent altercation which resulted in the victim's death."

Both of the defense attorneys shot to their feet, loudly objecting to State's Attorney Fenton's revisionist interpretation of the witness' testimony.

State's Attorney Fenton ignored them, increased the volume, and plowed on. "Further, during a visit to the defendant, Michael Franklin Early, at the county jail, the witness, Pastor Brady, saw a tattoo"—she jabbed her finger toward the photo—" on the defendant's arm and connected it to a specific cry for help the witness had heard the victim make on the morning the witness found him. This unique frozen cry indicated to Pastor Brady that the victim was telling him the identity of the man—the ONLY other person present that night—who inflicted the wound which most certainly caused his death.

Good God, Dave thought, *she knows how to bring a point home.*

Michael's attorneys were still on their feet, pleading with the bench for order as State's Attorney Fenton concluded her jackhammer assertions.

Silencing his gavel, Judge Cramer tossed it to the side and pointed his finger at the state's attorney. "Save it for your closing arguments, Counselor!"

State's Attorney Fenton was on her way to her seat before the verbal exchanges were completed. "Your Honor, I have nothing further," she said.

Chapter 14

He blinked. The light leaking into the bedroom from around the window shade betrayed the late hour. Dave leaned forward on his wife's side of the bed, which was empty, and saw the bright red numbers on the alarm clock. He flopped back down in disgust—7:05 a.m. Dave was normally in the parsonage eating breakfast after his walk by this time.

It took a few seconds for his mind to focus.

Good God! He bolted upright, simultaneously flipping the covers aside. His feet hit the floor with a thud. He had crawled between the sheets last night fretting about what he had said during yesterday's testimony, puzzling over what had really happened to Sonny, eventually dropping off to sleep in ignorance. Now, he knew—he was certain! The set of events leading to Sonny's death were crystal clear in his mind.

Powerless in the courtroom himself, Dave was seized by the urgency of contacting Michael's lawyers. He jumped out of bed. By the time Barb entered the bedroom to investigate the noise, he was rifling through his billfold in search of the business card Bill had given him. Business cards, notes, coupons, and cash were strewn all over the top of the dresser.

"What is going on?"

"Got to make a call!" Dave shouted.

"Now? It's not even eight o'clock yet," Barb's caution came in corresponding volume.

Without answering, Dave disappeared into the TV room and closed the door. He did not appear for a half hour. Throughout the following hour, his cell phone rang three more times, and for each call Dave escaped Barb's presence to answer.

Still a ball of nerves, he sat amidst the large mauve flowers strewn across the fabric that covered their sofa. His hands were leafing through a Time magazine, supposedly in search of an article of interest. His mind, which had left the parsonage an hour ago, was still at some location known only to himself.

Something, someone, was in front of Dave, had been in front of him, knowingly silent. He looked up and there was Barb still in her pink terrycloth robe and fluffy slippers, a sly grin gracing her lips. She passed the white coffee mug from her right to her left hand, then, broadening her grin, extended her hand toward him. "Hi, my name is Barb, I live here, and even though your brain is way off somewhere else, I just wanted you to know I love you and I understand."

Barb laughed. Dave, welcoming the diversion, smiled and then stood to embrace her.

Releasing the tight hug, Dave looked into his wife's face. "I'm so sorry, Barb."

"And I'm sorry about all this stress," she responded. "Are you okay?"

"Yes," he said. "This whole thing is so upsetting, and I thought of something overnight that really needs to be said in court, and I'm afraid—even after talking to the lawyers—that Michael's attorney's won't understand and won't ask the right questions."

"Do you want to talk about it?"

"No, actually, I wish I could take a walk—to clear my head—but it's too late for that."

"Why is it too late?" Barb asked. "You don't have to be in court until after lunch. Go ahead and take a walk."

A few minutes later, Dave—tucked back within himself—walked out the front door of the parsonage without the normal goodbye kiss for Barb.

* * *

The unique, clean odor of the courthouse interior filled Dave's nostrils at 12:45 p.m. His morning walk, though later than usual, helped him get through the early hours, and even get a little work done before he left for Gillespie. *"Please God, help me get this right,"* he said to himself, as he walked down the corridor toward the courtroom door.

To offer his testimony, however, he would have to wait, and wait, and wait! He was sequestered with a deputy in a side room until just after three. As he made his way to the courtroom door, he caught a brief glimpse of Tina and her parents as they were leaving the courtroom. They went the opposite direction and were unaware of his presence.

After Dave was seated in the witness chair, Judge Cramer reminded him he was still under oath, then asked if he needed water. Dave smiled, declined, as he was too distracted to realize he would need a sip of water later.

There were only four people in the visitors' gallery. A young man—he guessed a reporter—and Sandy and her parents. He nodded in their direction and smiled. Only Ralph returned the pleasantry. Sandy's hair was jumbled, and her mannerisms were in accord with the mess Dave knew she had to be on the inside.

Bill Early, the lawyer in training, offered his witness a smile as he began. "Pastor Brady, welcome back to the courtroom. I might also add your reputation as a man of integrity preceded you to the courtroom, and was also evident in the testimony you offered yesterday." The fledgling attorney's professional manner, carefully enunciated words, and confident tone, stood in contrast to his youthful high-pitched voice. *He'll have to work on that voice thing,* Dave thought.

"Pastor Brady," Bill fiddled with his tie, "I would also like to apologize for the delay in calling you in—setback could not be helped." The voice inflection and smile accompanying the last half of Bill's apology was suggestive. *They got it done,* Dave thought.

Bill paused for a moment. Mind now fully focused upon the court proceedings, Dave stopped his foot from spontaneously twitching. The defense attorney wrapped the fingers of his right hand around his chin—it looked awkward. "I would like to begin, Pastor, by reviewing your previous testimony."

Bill summarized Dave's discovery of the body, his entrances into Sonny's home, reiterated Dave's insistence he had seen no one present on or near the crime scene, and Dave's subsequent visits with the defendant at the Wabaunsee County Jail. On several points along the way, he requested conformation from the witness.

As Bill looked down at his papers, Dave glanced at Michael, who was seated beside Dr. Schultz at the defense table. Michael seemed distracted; he was looking down at the table and jiggling his feet. The foot movement ceased when Dr. Schultz placed his hand on Michael's arm.

Bill moved on. "Let's talk about the unique last outcry you heard on October twenty-fifth, the morning you found Sonny James Wigg in the snow. In your testimony yesterday, I believe you referred to it as a 'frozen scream.' Could you repeat the sound for us please?"

"Well, what I heard was 'adder,' but it was all drawn out like, 'aaaddderrr.'"

State's Attorney Fenton was seated at her table. She leaned forward, listening carefully, completely focused on the questioning. It reminded Dave of a cat, tail twitching, ready to pounce.

"Okay, Pastor." Bill motioned toward the photo of the defendant's tattoo, which was still perched on the tripod. "Your explanation of why you connected this tattoo with the victim's strange scream yesterday made no sense to me then, and still doesn't. Tell me again, how is this tattoo connected?"

"Well . . . um . . . when I heard Sonny's cry—I was right beside him—I didn't know what to make of it. I thought he was trying to say something. It wasn't just a scream. He was trying to say a word, and what I heard was something that sounded like 'adder.' I didn't think of a snake until I saw Michael's tattoo. The minute I saw the image on Michael's arm, the strange scream popped into my head. I thought it might be a nickname for Michael, the defendant, and that Sonny, in this cry, was trying to tell me who attacked him."

"The connection—the only connection—is the similarity in sound of the snake's name and the victim's cry. Correct?"

"Yes . . . there was no real thought to it. The idea came instantly as soon as I saw the tattoo."

The counselor raised an eyebrow in mock curiosity. "Did you try to confirm your hunch, or suspicion, or . . . whatever you want to call it?" His question was packaged in a flippant tone.

"Yes!" Dave answered. "I asked Michael if the snake in the tattoo was an adder. He didn't say anything in response. He didn't seem to know what I was talking about. I would have expected him to act that way though, even if what I thought was correct."

"Is that it? Is that all ya got?" Bill's high-pitched voice effectively conveyed sarcasm.

Good job, Counselor, Dave thought.

"Also, I asked Misty Wendell, and she said she had never heard Michael referred to as 'Adder,' just 'Red' or 'Big Red' because of his hair. She had also heard Sonny call Michael 'Flair' once because he lost his temper so easily. Later I happened to see Baunsee's town police officer, Greg Anderson, and asked if he'd heard Michael referred to as 'Adder,' but he just laughed at me and told me I had a great imagination."

At that point," Bill planted his index finger on the podium, "you no longer believed the victim's scream was an attempt to communicate something to you."

"Well, that's not quite true. I had doubts that adder, as in the snake, was what Sonny was trying to say to me, but I still had the feeling there was something Sonny wanted me to know."

"Before we move on, Pastor, let's put your unsubstantiated hunch to rest. As much as I respect you, your profession, and your professional integrity, without more evidence than you've offered us today, I must regard your 'gut feeling' as a fanciful suspicion that may well make a good film about 1920's Chicago or New York City, but does not fit the reality of an insignificant little town like, Baunsee, Illinois, in 2006. Do you have anything else to back up your assumption?"

"No," Dave said, concluding the matter with a shrug and sheepish grin.

Without even a glance down at his papers, Bill got to the defense team's crucial question: "What do you think that strange cry means now? Or does it mean anything at all, Pastor Brady?"

"Well, I'm quite sure the scream didn't mean what I initially thought when I saw the defendant's tattoo, but to explain what I've come to think now, I have to go back to when I visited the victim's mother, Ms. Tina Timkin. I already told you how I found the marijuana and was asked to—"

"Objection!" The state's attorney rose to her feet, extending her right hand toward the judge. "Yesterday we agreed to keep the content of the visit between Pastor Brady and the victim's mother confidential."

"Your Honor," Dr. Schultz stood. He had a puzzled look on his face. "Yesterday we agreed to keep the serious talk between Dave and the victim's mother confidential, not the discovery of the marijuana, which took place after the counseling session had ended."

The judge directed his gaze to Dave. "Pastor Brady, is your testimony going to involve the conversation between you and the victim's mother, Ms. Tina Timkin, or the discovery of the marijuana?"

"It's only about the marijuana, Your Honor."

"The defense may proceed."

"Please continue, Pastor," Bill said.

"Well, before I could look at the opening in the soffit of the Wigg home, where I—where Tina and I found the marijuana—we needed a ladder." Dave pointed to a ladder, which was on the floor perched lengthwise against the facing wall of the jury box. It was the decades-old ladder Tina's father had made.

"To remind the jury," Bill interrupted, "the ladder has already been entered into evidence. Please go on, Pastor."

"Tina told me that ladder had been stored on the ground along the side of their house for years. Her father had built it and stored it at his daughter's house so he wouldn't have to bring one when he came to clean out the rain gutters. On the afternoon when Tina and I found the marijuana, the ladder was gone. We looked all around the house and yard. Tina had phoned to see if her father had taken it, but he hadn't. The ladder had simply vanished!"

The jury stared at Dave, hanging on his every word.

Dave continued, "Tina looked down the gully behind her house and saw the ladder lying there. After we brought it up, I used the ladder to look in the place I surmised Sonny had hidden his marijuana. As I've previously testified, I found the Tupperware container of marijuana hidden inside a hole in the soffit."

"Your Honor, the container and marijuana contents were entered into evidence by the state's attorney," Bill said, as he nodded at State's Attorney Fenton, then turned his attention back to Dave. "So, Pastor Dave, what you said is interesting, but you'll have to explain what it has to do with this case."

"Well, I don't want anyone to think I was being deceptive when I gave my testimony yesterday. When I saw the tattoo on Michael's arm, Sonny's scream just jumped into my head. There was no conscious thought or reasoning to it—it just popped into my mind, and that's what I had told the state's attorney in a pre-trial interview. But when I was asked about the tattoo and the scream in court yesterday, there was something about my hunch that didn't seem right. A part of it, I suppose, is remembering how Greg Anderson, our village policeman, had laughed at me when I shared the hunch with him. At any rate, I had doubts but nowhere else to go to explain what Sonny, the victim, had meant by the scream."

Dave paused, swallowed, worried that his explanation was not coherent enough that the jury could understand what he was trying to say.

"After testifying yesterday," Dave continued, "I was confused about the whole thing."

Bill stopped him. "By the 'whole thing,' do you mean putting all of the things you knew, including the lost ladder, the marijuana, and the get-together of the defendant and victim into some logical explanation of what had happened on the night the defendant and the victim got together?"

"Your Honor," the state's attorney asserted, "the defense attorney is leading the witness."

"Sustained."

Bill was a bit shaken and took a few seconds to regain his composure. "Pastor, tell us what your confusion about the scream meant."

"I just couldn't put all of the pieces of the puzzle together—all the facts I knew—together in a way that could explain what happened to Sonny. Anyway, I couldn't sleep when I went to bed last night. I tossed and turned half the night. When I woke up this morning, however, I knew . . . I just knew! It had all come together in my mind. Everything—all of the pieces fit together—made sense. Every bit of the evidence I've heard supports what I now believe the victim's strange scream meant."

"So . . ." Bill folded his arms across his chest, and with knitted brow and narrowed eyes asked, "What does it all mean, Pastor? Enlighten us!"

"Michael didn't kill Sonny." Dave's voice was confident.

Michael, Sandy, and her family all sat up straight, their hope-filled eyes locked on Dave.

"Go on," Bill said, as he leaned over the lectern. "Fill us in! How does the scream make sense? What does the ladder have to do with the alleged crime?"

"The cry I heard had nothing to do with a snake, a nickname, or anything else relating to Michael," Dave said. "Sonny was trying to tell me what happened. Sonny put the ladder up against the house, climbed up, and fell. His final scream, his final word, was not 'adder' but 'ladder.' Sonny fell from the top of the ladder, pulling the ladder down with him."

The courtroom was dead silent.

"Okay, Pastor Brady." Bill's eyes, accompanied by a shrug, narrowed. "I'm still not clear on how you think this all went down."

"You see, sometime after Michael left—"

"Are you referring to the night the victim and defendant were together?" Bill interrupted.

"Yes," Dave responded. "After the fight at Sonny's house, I believe Michael, the defendant, took his game controller and left the house, just like he said. Afterward, Sonny started to hurt from the beating he'd taken, and he wanted marijuana to cope with the pain. He went outside to get it from his hiding place. He put the ladder against the house and climbed up, he then fell backward and hit his head on a stone in the yard. Maybe the same stone I tripped on!"

Bill lifted his hands. "Something is missing. How come the police didn't see the ladder? How did the ladder end up in the gully behind their house?"

"Sonny's backyard declines steeply into a deep vale, and along the bottom it's filled with trees and brush," Dave explained. "When the ladder fell, it hit the ground in such a way that it slid, just like a toy sled, right down into the valley. The morning I found Sonny, the ladder was down there, but nobody knew to look for it."

Bill's next question was a logical one. "They don't have a fence across their backyard, or bushes to stop something from sliding down?"

"No," Dave responded. "It's just an easy slope down to the brush and grove of trees along the creek bed. In Sonny's tumble to the ground, the ladder fell in the snow and slid right down into the valley. By the time it got light enough to see any tracks in the snow left by the ladder, the freshly falling snow had filled them in."

Dave looked at Michael. Big mistake. The defendant was crying. His mother and grandmother in the visitors' gallery were weeping as well. Against his will, the emotional cleric joined them, as always, cursing himself for his unwelcome emotional nature.

Dr. Schultz stood and requested a moment to consult with his co-counsel. The three of them—Dr. Schultz, Bill Early, and Michael—formed a huddle. Dave struggled to pull himself together.

When the short recess was concluded, Dr. Schultz was standing at the lectern. "Let me repeat this back to you, Pastor, to make sure the court understands what you have testified." His low, distinct voice was calm, each confident word enunciated with purpose.

Step by step, the seasoned attorney went through the timeline from the meeting of the two friends to play a computer game and smoke marijuana, to the death of the victim. At several points, Dr. Schultz questioned Dave about either the time-line or the meaning of some fine point in his testimony.

Dr. Schultz then addressed the court, "This morning, earlier today, you heard testimony from an expert witness that the massive damage to the back of the victim's head could not have been caused by a simple slip and fall to the ground, even if the victim's head struck a rock. The victim had to have hit the ground with a great deal of force. The testimony from this witness, backed up by solid evidence, is that the force was not inflicted by an angry assailant but by a fall from the top of a ladder. Sonny James Wigg was not attacked and thrown to the ground by our client, Michael Franklin Early, as the prosecution alleges, but fell from the top of a ladder, and the force of the fall smashed the back of his head against a stone in his yard, causing the intracranial hemorrhage, the brain bleed medical experts have attested to be the cause of his death.

Dr. Schultz turned his attention to the judge. "Your Honor, the evidence presented today, expert testimony, along with the testimony of this witness and two supporting witnesses, Miss Misty Wendell and Mrs. Tina Timkin, leads to the inescapable conclusion that the plaintiff, the State of Illinois, cannot possibly gain a conviction beyond a reasonable doubt in the second-degree murder charge against our client. We move for the dismissal, with prejudice, of the second-degree murder charge against Michael Franklin Early."

Chapter 15

The Speckled Sussex, a classy restaurant just outside of Peoria, had a warm atmosphere. The maître d' led Dave and Barb down the narrow hall and into a cozy back room where a table for two was tucked away in a quiet corner. It was early in the evening and there were few patrons. After finishing their Saturday afternoon shopping in Peoria, Dave was looking forward to a romantic evening with his wife.

They ordered wine, then looked over the menu in silence. There was nothing to entice Dave from his favorite house dish of prime rib—the large portion. He leaned back in his chair and sighed. He was tired and welcomed both the diversion of shopping and the seclusion of the restaurant's dimly lit back room.

"What a stressful week you had," Barb said quietly.

"What a stressful week we both had," Dave replied. "You had to put up with my grouchy disposition."

Barb smiled. "I'm used to it," she teased.

The waiter returned and placed a glass of wine before each of them. After placing their order, Dave held up his wineglass for a toast. "To a wonderful day together."

They clinked their glasses together and took a sip.

After his afternoon testimony yesterday, Dave couldn't stay for the ruling, so he'd left the courthouse and rushed to the hospital for a quick visit with a surgery patient. It all felt like a dream, if he were honest with himself. When he gave his testimony, he had the constant feeling that he wasn't telling it right, that he was not saying it so they could understand, and it was so important to him that the jury got the truth in a way they could understand it. Michael's future depended upon him and him alone. Barb had watched the six o'clock news and had told Dave the outcome as soon as he came in the door last night.

"I was ecstatic when I got home last night and you told me the murder charge against Michael was dismissed." Dave said, "I just can't get over it."

"I think they heard you scream with joy on the other end of town," Barb said exuberantly.

"I've tried to help so many troubled young people during my ministry," Dave continued, "and there's been so little certainty about the outcome of any of those efforts. But here, with Michael, it's crystal clear, for the whole world to see, that he's an innocent young man."

The other two tables were staring at them and Barb used hand gestures in an effort to get him to tamp down his volume.

"Thank God my testimony was clear enough that the judge understood and set Michael free." Dave lowered his voice to begin with, but unconsciously increased the volume as he spoke. "The outcome has been in the news broadcast, will be written up in the newspapers, and a part of the legal records at the courthouse for as long as that stately old building stands."

Dave forcibly pushed the tears of joy aside, compelled his quivering lips to smile, then held up his glass to offer the second toast of the evening. "God's justice," he said. "Freedom restored to an innocent young man."

"I want to hear the whole courtroom drama again," Barb said, and asked question after question about the proceedings while they took their time enjoying their favorite cuisine. Dave could sense that his lovely wife was relishing the opportunity to help him bask in a rare moment of genuine accomplishment. Dave welcomed her inquiries, even the repeated questions. She seemed to be especially interested in the pieces of the puzzle he had used to put what had really happened to Sonny all together.

Her plate nearly empty, Barb placed her napkin on the table. She leaned toward Dave and reached her hand across to him. "I am so proud of you," she said.

"All I did was tell the truth." He pushed back the tears once again as he took Barb's hand, squeezed it, and then took a moment to sit in silence and feel good about himself.

"So what happens to Michael now?" Barb looked more curious than concerned. "A high school dropout, a violent temper, doesn't have a job, does nothing but play computer games . . . not much promise in that. He's a troubled young man. Maybe you should step in and try to help him."

Dave grinned, released Barb's hand, and sat back in his chair. For some reason, he was having trouble reading Barb's suggestion. Was she being truthful, or was a part of her upset that he spent too much time on his ministry and helping others? "You don't need to worry about me seeing too much of Misty right now." Dave looked down at the table as he spoke. "She avoids me, hasn't called me in more than a month, skips out a back door when she comes to church."

"Is she mad at you for something?"

Of course she's mad, he thought. *When was Misty not angry?* But even though she was angry at him, he knew Misty was grateful for his friendship and guidance. Misty had a way of making things all about her, which seemed odd considering she was so private and guarded. But the wall she'd built around herself would eventually crack. She would trust Dave again—eventually. He just hoped that she would learn to trust others, to know that not everyone was out to get her.

"Misty is . . . Misty," he said. "She'll come around at some point, she always does."

Someone laughed at the nearby table, and Dave looked over. It was an elderly woman, with gray curly hair and wearing red lipstick. There was something about the laugh that reminded him of Sandy, Michael's mother. It felt forced, as if the woman was trying too hard to sound happy. When he'd talked to Sandy outside the convenience store, he remembered how strained her smile had been, a woman who was putting on a happy face for the world even though she was crumbling on the inside.

"I could certainly give Michael a call," Dave said, "and you can be sure that I will. We know each other now, and it's a great opportunity to step in. But I can't have an ongoing relationship with Michael unless he wants to further the relationship with me."

Troubled kids always seemed to confide in him. Maybe it was because they felt judged by every other adult in their life. Dave provided a clean slate for them to vent, but only if they were willing. He never pried into their personal matters.

He reached over and took Barb's hand. "I will contact Michael to see if I can help him any further," he said, "you can bet on that."

Barb smiled.

"It's been such a relaxing day and a celebration at the same time. I'm so glad we finally got some time together." Dave smiled.

"I've always understood your need to help troubled kids." Barb smiled again, but the smile was slowly replaced with a more serious look. "I just want you to be careful and consider what your efforts might look like to others."

"Regarding Michael, I think there's something else that might help you to know." Dave said, brushing aside Barb's caution. "The second time I went to see Michael in jail, it was just he and I, and we got beyond the gaming stuff and religion. Michael is intelligent. He can think straight when he needs to. He certainly has the potential to do some good for himself and make his mom proud. More important than that, I think this whole thing with Sonny has really set him on his heels. I would not be surprised to see him pull his act together."

Barb gently squeezed Dave's hand and used her other hand to down the last sip of her wine. "Yes, but will he?"

"He has a chance now," Dave said, "and that's all I have to give him."

"You did give him that chance, Dave. All I have to give him is prayer."

"Your part is the most important," Dave concluded. He retrieved his billfold, took out a credit card, and laid it atop the bill. They left the restaurant, arm-in-arm and pulled their jackets tighter around their necks as they stepped out into the cold night air.

It didn't take Dave's car long to warm up. He removed his gloves and stretched his hand toward Barb. She took it and held it tightly. It was too dark for him to see the satisfied look on his wife's face, but he knew it was there and relished it. Despite her fears concerning his ministry with troubled kids, their marriage was a happy one for him, and he saw all the signs that it was equally happy for her. He especially loved being with her in quiet moments like this.

Life couldn't get any better for Dave. He was married to his dream girl, and he had stood up for God's justice, and won! He would remember that victory until his dying day.

Epilogue

The combination of fall color and beautiful blue sky dotted with fluffy white clouds made it a great day for a drive through the countryside. While the grass in the ditches along the road remained green, the trees scattered among the now empty fields displayed the beautiful colors of autumn. Pastor Dave Brady, retired, and living some distance from Baunsee, had never lost his love for the sights and sounds of the Midwest.

Today, Dave was on a mission.

After negotiating an S-curve, he turned left to ascend a driveway up an embankment lined to one side with poplar trees sporting yellow-brown leaves. Entering the trailer park, he turned right on Bell Street. Ahead, he saw an attractive young woman wearing jean shorts and a wrinkled sleeveless cream top pushing an old reel lawnmower in a tiny section of yard.

"Good Lord," he said to himself. "Jasmine? I can't believe it!"

She recognized him as soon as he stepped out of the car, and just like she had as a child, ran to him and threw her arms around him.

A lined yellow notepad in one hand, Dave returned the affection with his free arm. Phyllis came out onto the small porch. She was as thin as a rail. She had an oxygen tube in her nose as well as a mid-sized green oxygen canister on wheels. Gasping for breath, she leaned to rest her elbows on the two-by-four railing.

Dave, still wearing a smile, released Jasmine and moved toward the wheelchair ramp.

"Misty's comin'," Jasmine called after him.

Dave beamed his approval. "Good, I'd love to see her." He thought she would come.

Dave put one arm around Phyllis, who was too exhausted to make any response. "I'm so sorry, Phyllis," he said, as a light breeze ruffled the sleeve of her housecoat just below his hand.

When she caught her breath, she looked up, and in her familiar gruff voice, volume so low he could barely hear, said, "I did it to myself . . ." She went on, but whatever she said had so little volume Dave could make out just one word, "cigarettes."

Inside the trailer, Dave sat on one of the benches of the built-in table. Jasmine sat a mug of steaming coffee before him. Phyllis, in her wheelchair, had pulled up to the outside edge. At the dying woman's insistence, her former pastor had come out of retirement to plan her funeral service.

"Misty called and said she'd be late," Jasmine said, as she laid her cell phone on the table. "She doesn't want you to leave till she sees ya." Her voice had matured, a lower tone, like her mother, but without the raspy quality to it. "She's really changed," the younger sister continued, "you'll be surprised."

"Well, a year or so before I left Baunsee, she quit school and went to live with an older guy—if I remember correctly."

"Right." Jasmine looked at her mom, wondering if she should fill in the details. Phyllis placed her hand on Jasmine's wrist, then said something so weak Dave couldn't hear it.

Jasmine looked at Dave through her pretty brown eyes, leaned toward him, and in an earnest tone, she said, "But she's different now . . . everything has changed. She's doing good, got married, and even got her GED!"

Dave grinned. "Great! What happened?"

Phyllis lifted her hand to block Jasmine from responding.

"Mom wants Misty to tell ya." There was an awkward pause. "How about Mom's service?" She looked over at her Mom as the emotion-laden words left her lips.

Dave took the pen from his shirt pocket and moved the yellow note pad into position. "You don't want to wait for Misty to get here?"

Both women shook their heads. "Mom told me what she wanted," Jasmine said. "Mainly for you to do the service."

It was to be a simple grave side ceremony and didn't take long to plan. The most lengthy part involved a concluding discussion about faith and undying divine love, with special emphasis on the assurance of God's forgiveness.

The plans for the service were completed with a prayer, and the three launched into a discussion of what was going on in Baunsee, and with the people they knew there. Not long after their gossip session began the front door opened—a female hand, judging from the polished nails, held the door open. In rushed a tow-headed little boy who didn't stop until he had planted himself in the widespread arms of Jasmine.

Misty walked in right behind him, one arm holding a medium-sized brown paper sack full of groceries to her chest. Dave stood to greet her as she, with a broad smile, ignored him and went to the kitchen counter to relieve herself of the sack. Turning toward him, she displayed the same bobbed haircut, dimples still in the center of each cheek, and an attractive but mature face. She had slimmed down and looked the picture of health.

The two greeted each other with a couple of tight hugs for emphasis. Misty stepped back to look at him. "You haven't changed a bit!"

"You have," Dave said. "You're all grown up!"

Arm in arm, Misty swivelled to introduce her five-year-old. "This is my son, Aiden. Aiden, say hi to Pastor Dave." The boy covered his eyes with his arm as he turned and buried his face into Jasmine's chest.

The reunion of the four didn't last long. Phyllis was exhausted and had to go lie down. Jasmine and her adorable nephew went outside to find something more fun to do. That left Misty and Dave to talk.

Saying nothing of the embarrassing years, Misty filled him in on what had happened in her life. She had been floundering and gave birth to Aiden. She began her story with her job at a country bar just outside of Gillespie. There she had met a farmer, a man old enough to be her father. A year earlier, his wife had died of cancer and he was lonely. She fended off his advances at first, but there was something special about him. She came to believe he wanted her, not just her body, and Aiden and he adored each other. They were married just over two years ago.

Steve was a stable person. He owned a farm, and he was going to help with the funeral expenses for Phyllis. Despite the age difference, even in admitting some difficulties in the relationship, Misty seemed happy, talked spontaneously, and was content in a way Dave had never seen her. She was, indeed, a transformed young woman.

When Dave was ready to leave, Misty walked him to his car. She leaned against the driver's side door so he couldn't get in. "Do you remember after I quit school and left Baunsee when you came to see me at the hospital?"

"Yes," he said, their backs now side by side against the driver's side door of the car. "I remember it all very well." Misty couldn't help but note the voice inflection, which was accompanied by a "knowing" smile.

"What's that supposed to mean?"

"What?" Dave said, his face coated in feigned innocence.

"The silly grin."

"Well, you had fallen down a set of stairs and lost a baby. That part wasn't funny. I was sorry then, and I'm sorry now. But I don't know what kind of pain med or whatever they had you on in the hospital, but you were . . . talkative."

"Oh God! What did I tell you?" Misty covered her crimson face with her hands.

"Well, let's put it this way: I learned a whole lot about your lifestyle in Gillespie."

Misty doubled up her fist and smacked him in the shoulder, hard, just like she did when she was younger.

Dave rubbed his shoulder and smiled. "What do you want to say, Misty?"

Misty turned toward him and placed her elbow on the roof of the car. "Well, when I look back on it, it just seemed, even when I was mad at you for something and didn't want you around, when I got in trouble you were there. I could always depend on you, and even when you got angry, you did it in a kinda gentle way. That's how Steve is. Even when I try to push him away, and I'm sorry to say I've done that, when I need him he's there, and he has the same kind of gentle way of approaching things. It makes me feel like he really loves me, and I really love him."

Dave responded with a broad smile.

"We go to church," she said, "all of us, regularly. I'm a Sunday School teacher now, not just a helper, like in Baunsee."

What she said about her husband moved her former pastor, bringing a lump to his throat.

Misty wrapped her arms around his neck and drew him down for a kiss on the cheek but didn't let go. She laid her head on his chest and whispered, "He's like you, Pastor Dave, kind of gentle, and no matter how hard I tried to push him away, he never gave up or rejected me—never let me go. That is real love!"

On the way home, Dave watched the colorful Midwest autumn countryside fly by, relishing the clear sky and brightly colored leaves. He cried and felt no shame—no shame at all.

Postscript

Tribute to a Third Grade Teacher

The busy hallway was filled with elementary school students. The walls were plastered with art projects and colorful paintings of zoo animals and letters of the alphabet. When the third-grade boy entered his classroom, leaving the noise of the busy hallway behind, he made his way into the cloakroom to hang his gray coat. As he made his way to his desk a girl wearing a purple dress smiled at him and said, "Good morning." But the anxious boy—his mind a million miles away—remained silent as he passed by.

After reciting the Pledge of Allegiance, the teacher seated her class and turned their attention to yesterday's homework assignments. Thankfully, the boy's mom had helped him complete the math problems on the mimeographed take-home paper long before his father stumbled home from the tavern.

The teacher walked through the five rows of desks, checking the students' math homework and giving them back their writing assignment from the week before. The room was filled with an electric energy as the students chatted and laughed. But the boy stared out the window, prevented from participating in the lighthearted fun of his classmates by a mind filled with vivid memories of the horrible argument his mother and intoxicated father had the night before.

Then the murmurs of the class quieted down until it was silent.

Abruptly, the boy was wrenched back to the present by the sound of his name being spoken in an uncharacteristically positive tone. Everyone was staring at him. The boy looked down and saw his handwriting on the lined pages—words written in cursive, with loopy consonants and vowels—a magical story he'd written. The teacher was praising his short story, her carefully chosen words of acclaim piling one upon another. His classmates smiled and cheered him for a job well done.

In that moment, a public school teacher lifted a tortured elementary child above the mental, emotional, and physical abuse that permeated his life at home, and offered him a glimpse of what he could make of himself. That incident would not be forgotten.

* * *

Much of that story about the boy is fictitious. The specific details of that incident left my mind a long time ago. What is not invented, and has not been forgotten, is that I am the product of a troubled home, and I wrote a short story in third grade that was praised before the entire class by my teacher. It was just what I needed that day, and lovingly offered to me by a teacher who sensed my distraught situation and provided an emotional Band-Aid that was just the right size and shape.

Unfortunately, I cannot remember that teacher's name, but the positive seed that she'd planted took root and quietly grew over the years, and when its time came, it pestered me until I began to write what I hoped to turn into a mystery novel.

As a career pastor, throughout my years in ministry I wrote religious essays and articles that were printed in a variety of Christian publications and local newspapers. As a part of my profession, I learned to enjoy writing and relished the delight of seeing something I had written in print. Those accomplishments, however, did not seem to fulfill the dreams of an eight-year-old boy—both the dream of writing fiction, and the desire to pay tribute to the person who originally lit that fire within me.

Throughout this country's history, there have been, and still are, countless public school teachers who care about their students, and who are perceptive enough to sense when their students need to be elevated in a positive light and step in at just the right moment. My third-grade teacher was there for me when I needed her, and even though I didn't know how to respond appropriately to her praise at the time, she added something to my dark world that continued to bring light.

In this thank you, I am confident that I don't stand alone. There have been many of us—hundreds, perhaps even thousands—a myriad of young spirits elevated to unimagined heights and accomplishments. Why? Because public school teachers in this country care and want to be there for their students, especially those who, for one reason or another, are facing otherwise insurmountable hurdles.

This piece is a tribute to a particular third-grade teacher employed by the public school system in Clarion, Iowa, in the mid-1940s. I assume she is no longer with us. Her words, however, remain in my heart, have given me hope throughout the years, and were the first and most influential impetus for writing my debut mystery novel, *Legacy of a Frozen Scream*.

A simple thank you is not enough to adequately compensate my teacher for what she did for me. I hope that wherever she is, she knows that her deeply troubled elementary student grew up and wrote a book.

Associated Writings

by Daniel D. Doty

"Canoe Outing Brings Youth Together." *Rock Island Argus*. September 29, 1985.

"Christ or Javier." *The Presbyterian Outlook*, volume 179, no. 43 (December 29, 1997).

"It's Still a Great Dream." *The Presbyterian Outlook*, volume 183, no. 2 (January 15, 2001).

"Laura, Society Messed Up Miserably." *Moline Dispatch*. September 28, 1987.

"Reflections of an Alcoholic's Son." *The Restoration Herald*. Published anonymously by the Christian Restoration Association, Cincinnati. June 1979.

"Relationships Are at Heart of After School Program." *Moline Dispatch*. January 15, 1998.

"The Best Christmas Gift of All." *The Presbyterian Outlook,* volume 181, no. 42 (December 20, 1999).

Made in the USA
Middletown, DE
15 September 2022